The City of
Epicantor

STRATOS MOUNTAINS

TITAN STRAITS

FAELE

RON STEPPES

EMERALD FALLS

The City of
Athelos

WASTELAND WILDERNESS

BITTERBOON
MOUNTAINS

Book 6

This book offers the reader the opportunity to read words with prefixes that relate to prepositions, such as 'super'.

Contents

Chapter 1: A Pleasant Surprise

The Quadrator carried them quickly away from the Misty Steps. It was an uncomfortable night, riding across a windswept, rocky terrain. They were glad when morning arrived. The Quadrator stopped at the top of a cliff.

"We will see each other again," he told them, as they clambered off his back. He pawed the ground impatiently, already gazing into the horizon. He was keen to be gone. "The time for battle is drawing closer," he told them as he galloped away.

They gathered together on the windy cliff top. Finn was holding the map. He pointed down to a sandy beach way below them. "That's where we need to go!" he told Izzy. They could see sunlight sparkling like diamonds on the blue sea.

Izzy laughed with relief. "At last, this quest has taken us somewhere beautiful!" she grinned.

Finn was not so sure. "It's odd, Izzy," he said with a frown. "The next monument looks as if it's actually in the sea."

Izzy pointed to a faint blue image of a spiral shining in the orb. The images were not always  easy to translate into clues. Finn tried to make sense of this one. A spiral? Was it a coiled snake? They didn't want to face another one of those!

"Over here!" yelled Kit. He had been searching for a route down to the beach. "This path looks safe," he called. He used his rope to help Finn and Izzy down a twisting pathway carved into the cliff face.

Izzy watched Kit and Monk climb confidently down the path behind her.

"Kit, you really are more goat than boy!" she joked. "Are you sure you're not one of these hybrid Guardians?"

It was a long way down. At last they arrived at the beach and stepped onto soft sand.

"Race you to the water!" yelled Kit. He and Finn were soon at the edge of the sea. Kit bent down and splashed Finn.

"I'll get you back for that!" yelled Finn. "Help me out, Izzy!"

Izzy was standing silently at the edge of the sea. She was gazing with wide eyes out at the water.

Chapter 2: A Strange Structure

What had Izzy seen? The boys peered out into the sea. An unusual structure was now visible in the sea. As the tide went out, more and more of it emerged from the water. Within minutes, a huge stone head was revealed. Was the rest of the statue buried in the sandy sea bed?

Finn's eyes were wide with excitement. "I think that's the next monument!" he gasped.

They splashed out to the strange new monument. The rock was crumbling with age and the sea water made it slippery. It was difficult to climb.

Eventually they managed to clamber on. Monk chattered excitedly. He had discovered some strange images carved into the stone. Finn bent down to look more closely. He tugged a web of seaweed off the stone. "There're words here too," he said. *"Here there be serpents,"* he read slowly. He stopped to look up at Kit.

"I don't want to imagine what that might mean," he said nervously.

Kit was keen to start exploring. "There's a hidden door here," he gasped. "A door is more important than some old sign. Can you help me open it, Finn?"

Izzy clambered up to the top of the strange statue. She glanced down at the orb as she climbed. She was hoping it would show them where to find the next jewel.

Izzy reached a stone centerpiece at the very top of the statue. Below her feet was a beautiful image of a sea creature. It was carved into the stone. "Now that is interesting," breathed Izzy. She bent down to look at it. As she knelt down, her foot brushed against the figure's eye.

There was a terrifying cracking sound. A huge crack opened up in the exact spot where the eye in the carving had once been! One minute Izzy was standing on solid stone, and the next she was plummeting into thin air! She dropped into a spiraling tunnel, deep inside the statue. There was no time to try and grasp at the tunnel's slippery walls. Screaming in shock, Izzy slid along it, then shot out into nothingness!

"That's Izzy's scream!" yelled Kit. They raced up to the top of the statue. A huge dark opening now filled the space where Izzy had been standing.

Monk dropped from Finn's shoulder and peered fearfully into the hole. Bending down, Finn could just hear Izzy's screams. She was far below them, deep inside the statue.

"I think she's fallen into some sort of internal tunnel!" Finn shouted in horror.

Chapter 3: The Underground Lake

There was an echoing splash from deep inside the statue. Then silence. They could no longer hear Izzy. The only sound was the wind whistling eerily around them.

Finn gazed fearfully at Kit. They didn't dare imagine what might have happened to Izzy. There was no time to lose if they were going to save her. The boys didn't need to talk about it.

"That's Izzy screaming," Finn told Monk grimly. "We're going in!" He tucked the tiny monkey deep inside his tunic. They lowered themselves slowly into the hole. Seaweed lined the walls of the slimy tunnel. It was impossible to keep a grip on it. Within seconds, they too were sliding deep down into the abyss.

Finn tried to grab Kit's arm as they rocketed through the inky nothingness. "Hang onto me, Kit!" he yelled. "We mustn't lose each other in the dark!"

It was too late. Within seconds they had hit the water. They had splashed heavily into the water, deep inside the huge statue.

"Tread water!" gasped Kit, as the boys surfaced. "We must find Izzy."

A sudden scream interrupted them. It was Izzy! Her voice echoed across the underground cavern. "Kit! Finn! I'm over here!"

The boys could just make out Izzy's profile in the gloom. She was clinging to a small rocky island.

They swam quickly through the water towards her. Even from a distance the island was unsettling. It seemed to be made of chunks of strange green rock. As they got closer, Finn could see trails of transparent slime welding the rocks together.

They clambered onto the island. It towered above them, the green rocks twisting in spiky coils. Finn peered down. More of the coiled trails of rocks were submerged under the water.

"Let's try and climb it!" said Kit. He swung his grapple against the rocks. Now they could use his rope to help them up.

It was not easy climbing up the island's

glassy surface. Kit showed them how to transfer their weight carefully from foot to foot to avoid slipping.

Suddenly the island gave a mighty shudder! It seemed to be shifting position in the water.

"Don't move!" hissed Izzy in terror. "I have a horrible feeling this island is not what it seems!"

Chapter 4: Living Island

Rippling movements in the rocks around them confirmed all their fears. This was no ordinary island. Kit grabbed Monk and held him close as they clung to the shuddering rock face.

A sudden jolt made Izzy stagger. The orb tumbled from her pocket! "Grab it, Finn!" she screamed, but it was no use. The orb hung in the air for a split second, then splashed loudly into the water below them!

An instant later, the whole island began to move! "The island is alive, Izzy," yelled Finn. "Hang on to it or you'll be dragged under the water!" Part of the island was indeed a living beast. It reared up out of the water. It transformed into the terrifying coils of a living serpent!

The serpent's massive head towered over them. Slime dripped from its jaws. What should they do? Kit and Izzy were transfixed with horror. They clung to the remaining rocks of the

collapsing island.

Finn had a different idea. Throwing himself off the serpent's back, he plunged into the water. He was desperately searching for the orb in the churning water.

Finn was trying hard to overcome his fear of being underwater. He knew his breath would not last long. There was no time to waste. He powered through the murky water towards the seabed. Surely the orb would have landed there?

Strange plants lined the seabed. Some of them seemed almost luminous. Bobbing plants shot out jolts of intermittent light that helped guide Finn through the murky water. Just ahead of him was a web of seaweeds. The green strands were interwoven so tightly that they had created a natural net. Finn's heart hammered in his chest with excitement. The orb was caught safely in the net of weeds!

Finn grabbed the orb and rammed it safely into his tunic. A dark mass rippled above him. It could only be one thing. The serpent! The air in Finn's lungs was running out. He needed to surface, but he could not risk coming out of the

water anywhere near that demon. He gathered the last of his strength and swam away from the serpent's snapping jaws. A sudden light distracted him. Ahead of him was a light-filled portal! He forced his aching body to swim towards it.

Chapter 5: Seeking Shelter

Above the water, things were not going well. Izzy and Kit tried desperately to stay afloat on the collapsing island. Monk was beside himself with fear after seeing Finn plunge into the water.

"I know, Monk," soothed Izzy. "Finn will get the orb and come back." A sudden light caught her eye. Something else had joined them in the water. It was a boat! In it were two dark spies!

"They must have realized the serpent was awake!" yelled Kit. "They've come looking for us, Iz. We have no choice. We have to follow Finn!"

There was no time to plan. They took a deep breath and dropped into the water.

The water was freezing. Izzy twisted around, trying to spot Monk and Kit. A flash of silvery light beneath her made her look down. Were they underneath her?

Underneath, it was an amazing underwater mosaic! She and Kit both gazed down at it.

The carpet of tiny marble tiles was beautiful. Not one of the tiny tiles was broken. Maybe the amber jewel would be inside it? Izzy knew only the Guardian in the amber jewel could save them from the serpent. She was just preparing to dive deeper into the water when a familiar face swam into view. It was Finn!

Finn led them through the water. He knew they would all soon be out of breath. He had to get them to the portal of light.

Finn dragged his weary friends through the portal of light. Within seconds, they were bursting out of the water and into an air pocket. They had arrived at a tiny underground cave. Izzy sobbed with joy as she breathed sweet fresh air into her aching lungs. Monk was exhausted from the swim. He clung weakly to Kit's back.

The three friends gazed below them at the strange plants. "If only my dad could see this!" gasped Izzy. Her eyes were wide with astonishment as she tried to make sense of the incredible plants around them. "There are plants down here he has never even dreamed about!"

A sudden shuddering interrupted them. Something hard and heavy was hitting the outside of the cave. The cave walls shuddered.

Finn pointed above them in horror. Tiny cracks were spreading like a web across the ceiling of the cave. "We have to go back out!" he yelled. "The cave won't survive this!"

"Follow me!" urged Izzy. She knew they had to get to the mosaic and find the amber jewel.

Chapter 6: Under Attack

Finn tucked Monk into his tunic as they swam back out through the portal.

The serpent could sense their movement. The horrifying coils of his body rippled through the water towards them. They needed to distract him away from the mosaic.

Izzy glanced up. There was a shadow on the surface of the water above them. It was the dark spies in their boat! Izzy began to swim up towards it, signaling for the others to follow her. If she could get the serpent to churn the water, he might topple the boat. That would keep all the enemies out of the way!

The serpent surged through the water behind the three desperate swimmers. They reached the surface and bobbed up out of the water, right next to the boat.

"Take a deep breath, and then swim back down!" yelled Izzy.

The serpent's massive head reared up out of the water. It was so close to them. For a moment, it seemed as if all was lost. Its eye glistened as it pulled itself up, ready to attack. When it lunged at them, it accidentally smashed the boat, sending the dark spies tumbling into the sea. Finn heard the wooden boat begin to splinter. He had no time to turn round and look. Gasping a deep breath, he dived back down into the water.

The three of them swam back down into the murky depths of the water. Where was the mosaic? Izzy scanned the water in panic. It was impossible. The thrashing tail of the sea serpent had swept up clouds of sand from the bottom of the sea. They would never find the mosaic again in this murky gloom.

Suddenly the orb shuddered in Finn's pocket. He tugged it out. It was glowing! Jolts of intermittent light flashed from inside it. They gave just enough light to see. Finn held it in front of him, swimming hard with his other arm.

The light from the orb picked up a sudden flash of amber. It was way down below them. Kit swam towards it. The orb flashed again. There it was again! A glint of light came from the seabed. Kit motioned to the others to follow him. It was the mosaic!

The mosaic was immense. Tiny squared tiles had been used to create a superb image of a

sea dragon. As Finn approached it with the orb, the dragon's eye began to glow softly. It was the amber jewel!

Kit sped through the water. Hovering above the mosaic, he tried to hack the amber jewel out with his ax. It was no good. It was stuck in the mosaic.

Chapter 7: Desperate Measures

Things were getting desperate. They were all exhausted and rapidly running out of air. Added to that, they had no hope of getting the amber jewel without help. Finn's heart jumped in his chest as he had a sudden idea. There was only one thing down here with the power they needed to shift the amber jewel! Swimming up above the mosaic, he began to twist about in the water. His plan worked. Within seconds, the coils of the sea serpent were rippling through the water towards him. Finn had made himself into human bait.

The serpent's powerful gaze was locked onto Finn. Spinning round, Finn began to swim back down towards the mosaic. Izzy and Kit were watching from below. They didn't understand his plan, but they could see how tired he was. He was swimming more and more slowly, dragging his weary limbs through the water. And the serpent was gaining ground.

The serpent was very close now. It opened
its huge jaws and lunged towards Finn. Izzy sped
up through the water. She pulled Finn's body
out of the way. Kit swam directly in front of the
serpent's glistening eye. The serpent could not
watch everything at once. It twisted in the water,
trying to keep track of all three of the swimmers.
Its powerful tail thrashed against the mosaic. It
dislodged the amber jewel! Finn grabbed the
jewel and slammed it into the orb.

Dazzling white light bleached the water. A beautiful Sea Dragon emerged from it. She swam towards them. The three friends grabbed hold of her mane.

The Sea Dragon raced through the water and out of the monument. She flew up into the sky. Finn grinned in relief when he heard Monk's chattering from inside his tunic.

The great Sea Dragon flew onwards. Izzy pointed down. "Well, we didn't get to spend any time on that beautiful beach!" she said.

Kit interrupted her. "This quest is about finding the amber jewels, not relaxing in the sunshine!" he reminded her with a grin.

Glossary

centerpiece – something placed in the center of something for decoration or because it is special

dislodge – remove or force out

emerged – came into view

hack – cut or chop roughly

hybrid – something bred from two different breeds or species

intermittent – stopping and starting, on and off

internal – inside

interwoven – woven together

luminous – shining and bright, lit up

murky – dark and gloomy

onward – moving forward

portal – door, gate or entrance

splinter – break up into small pieces

submerged – hidden or covered under something

transfer	– move something from one place or person to another
transfixed	– frozen, unable to move
transformed	– changed its appearance
translate	– turn from one language into another
transparent	– see-through
unsettling	– causing doubt or uncertainty

Facing Fears

Book 7

This book offers the reader the opportunity to read words with prefixes that relate to size, such as 'magna', 'mini' and 'micro'.

Contents

Chapter 1: Into the Clouds

Being on the back of the Sea Dragon felt like riding a storm! The Guardian sped away from the coast and straight up into the sky. Soon the beach was so tiny they could barely see it.

"That last monument looks miniscule from up here!" yelled Kit.

Izzy did not answer him. She was crouched low over Monk, sheltering his tiny body from the wind. He lay oddly quiet and still. "I'm not sure Monk has recovered yet from being underwater for so long," Izzy told Finn anxiously.

Finn was also feeling worried. They had flown so high that they were now traveling through the clouds. He had asked the Sea Dragon where she was heading, but had got no reply. It seemed almost as if the Guardian had forgotten they were there.

"Where are we going?" Finn yelled across to Kit. Kit shrugged, his eyes filled with excitement.

At that moment, a startling vision appeared before them. The top of an enormous mountain emerged through the clouds! Craggy rocks were covered with dense green plants. Waterfalls flowed among the rocks.

At the center of this strange new landscape was a magnificent stone head. A familiar golden glint shone from above one sunken eye socket. Was it the amber jewel?

The Sea Dragon was heading straight for the stone head. She circled in the air and landed skillfully on a rocky ledge just above it. Izzy cradled Monk as the three friends climbed carefully off the Sea Dragon's back.

The Sea Dragon still did not speak. She gave them one last scornful look as she prepared to leave. A cloud of dust and grit whirled around them as she took to the skies.

Izzy was tired and irritable after their underwater battle with the sea serpent. Anxiety

made her fear of heights worse than usual.

"Where are we?" she yelled after the Sea Dragon. "Are you just going to abandon us on this mountain?"

The Sea Dragon did not look back. She flew away from them, her magnificent wings spread wide. Soon she was just a microscopic dot on the horizon. They were on their own.

Chapter 2: Peril in the Sky

The mountain they were standing on was so high that the top of it reached right through the clouds. There was no sign of the land way below them.

"It feels like another world," Finn murmured to Izzy. He wasn't sure yet whether he felt excited or terrified.

Izzy was pale and tense. She and Monk stood well back from the edge of the rocky ledge they had landed on. The last thing she wanted to do was look down!

Finn grinned. "It'll be OK, Iz," he said kindly. "We'll find the next jewel and move on. At least there are no serpents up this high!"

Kit suddenly whooped with excitement. He had discovered a cloth bag filled with ropes and strange loops of metal. He held up a handful of them. "Finn!" he yelled. "It seems I'm not the only climber up here. Look at all this gear!"

Before Finn could answer, he was startled by a

sudden movement in the bushes behind them.
It was hard to see clearly. Was it a creature?
A strange figure emerged from the rocks. It was
hard to tell if the gray figure walking towards
them was really human. As she reached them,
she held up one arm.

"You must leave," she said nervously. "You
bring the threat of great danger with you."

The creature introduced herself as Maxine. "You can't stay here," she urged Finn. "You put our community in danger!"

Kit interrupted her. "We won't stay long," he said kindly. "We're on a quest. The thing we are searching for is in the eye socket of that amazing stone head. We will leave as soon as we have it."

Maxine had no chance to reply. A terrifying screeching sound echoed across the sky as a horde of winged beasts suddenly descended on them!

A dark cloud of beating, leathery wings filled the dark sky as the creatures drew closer. They skimmed close to the ground, their huge wings churning up clouds of roots and rocks. The creatures raced towards Maxine and the three friends, spitting and snarling.

"Follow me!" yelled Maxine. She turned and fled, with the others close on her heels.

The rocky top of the mountain seemed to be

covered in dense undergrowth. Finn searched wildly for a means of cover.

Kit had spotted something. There was a shelter of some sort hidden among the trees. It had been carefully designed to look like a bushy plant. Kit thought he could make out a door! His hopes were confirmed when the door was suddenly thrown open.

A wave of light burst from the open doorway. It surged over their heads and dazzled the creatures. The three friends raced towards the doorway. They just managed to hurl themselves through it as it slammed shut.

They were inside a tunnel. A mass of curious figures surrounded them. They were holding devices that fizzed with a strange energy. It was hard to tell at first if they were friendly.

Maxine took Izzy's hand. "Don't be alarmed," she said kindly. "We are the Evioli. We have lived hidden among the clouds, on the tip of this mountain, for centuries. We have always been a peaceful race. Those creatures outside came here searching for something. Until now we had no idea what it was."

"The amber jewel," murmured Izzy. She quickly explained their quest as Maxine led them through a series of spiraling tunnels. Eventually they reached a tall chamber, filled with the

strange metal devices.

Kit's eyes lit up. "Are they the source of that light?" he asked Maxine.

Maxine nodded. "The creatures hate strong light," she told him. She handed Kit one of them. "Keep it with you. If the creatures return, you may need it."

They were now deep inside the mountain top. The three friends were stumbling with exhaustion. "You are safe here," said Maxine softly. She pointed to a row of bunks. "Sleep now and recover your strength. We'll talk again in the morning."

Chapter 3: Forming a Plan

Finn woke up and gazed around him. The gloomy chamber was now filled with rays of hazy sunlight. He leaped out of his bunk. It was morning. They needed to get back to the quest!

"Kit! Izzy! Wake up!" he urged. "Those creatures don't like the bright sunlight. It's our best chance to get to the amber jewel."

They found Maxine near the exit of the cave. "Finn is right," she said. "Those creatures do tend to avoid the light. Take great care, though. If they are searching for the amber jewel, they will be close behind you. Recently they have been joined by a creature much larger than them. We have not seen it, but the shadow of it sometimes hovers high above them. When it is here, they fight even more violently."

She showed them how to operate the unusual light device she had given them yesterday. "It is powered by the energy of the sun," she explained.

"It will not last forever, so use it wisely."

Maxine unlocked the exit portal to let them out.
"There is another thing you must remember," she
said as they left. "Those creatures have incredible
hearing. If they are searching for you, then you
must keep any noise to an absolute minimum."

They stepped out into a cave filled with deep shadows. Finn gazed out across the clouds. The sun was rising on the other side of the mountain. Soon there would be even more light.

Kit looked around him. "This cave is in the mouth of the statue!" he whooped. "We only have to get up to the eye. This next jewel is going to be easy to find!" He was already busy putting together the climbing gear he had found when they arrived.

Izzy frowned. "Easy, Kit?" she asked crossly. "Do you think clambering up a stone head halfway up a massive mountain is easy?"

"I'm sorry, Izzy," said Kit. "I sometimes speak before I think. We are high up and we must be careful." He pointed out at the sky. "The sun is rising and we have Maxine's device. That will maximize our chances of avoiding those creatures."

He threw a grapple up at the eye of the statue. It caught in the eye socket and held firm.

Finn turned to Izzy. "Stay close to Kit and me," he told her gently. "I promise we won't let you fall."

The three friends clung to the rope. They began to clamber across the weather-beaten surface of the statue's face. Monk had recovered after a good night's sleep. He scrambled around them, chattering excitedly.

Chapter 4: The Face of Fear

It was a terrifying climb. The wind battered the three friends. It took all their concentration not to fall.

Eventually, Finn reached the statue's nose. He leaned down to help Izzy up. "The eye socket isn't far now!" he told her.

Izzy was exhausted. The curved nostril of the statue's nose was a safe ledge to rest on. "I'll wait here," she told Finn. "We need to come back this way anyway. You and Kit go ahead and find the jewel."

Kit was a fantastic climber. He and Monk clambered up to the eye socket with minimal effort. Finn was just behind him. "Have you found it?" he panted.

"It's nowhere to be found," said Kit. "It's really strange – I'm sure I saw it in the left eye socket, but there's no trace of it at all."

Finn groaned in frustration. "This is the right eye, Kit! You've muddled up your left and right again!"

Kit often got his left and his right confused. Usually it didn't matter, but this climb had taken all their strength. He peered across the statue's face to the other socket. "It's OK, Finn. We won't need to go back. We can climb across here."

Kit looped the rest of their rope through his grapple. He hurled it across to the other eye socket.

They began to edge carefully across the statue's stone nose. The wind howled in their ears like a wild beast. Finn was halfway across when the light suddenly dimmed. It was as if a huge shadow had crossed in front of the sun.

"Keep going, Finn!" yelled Kit. "You're halfway there now."

Finn struggled to see the way ahead in the gloomy light. The shadow grew even darker and the noise of the wind suddenly changed. Finn glanced above him. It was not just the sound of the wind he could hear. Above him was a huge cloud of the winged creatures!

Finn lost his grip on the stone. He was clinging to the edge of the statue's stone nose. His feet swung wildly in the air. The creatures did not waste any time. Hissing with spite, they

began to attack!

Above them, a fresh horde of snarling creatures launched themselves at Kit. He ducked his head to avoid them as he tried desperately to reach out to Finn.

Chapter 5: Desperate Measures

Finn swung his feet towards the stone face, grasping for a foothold in the rough stone. The shrieking creatures grabbed at him with razor-sharp claws. Their nails grazed his skin as he fought to keep hold of the statue.

At last, Finn managed to get a foothold on the stone. He began to claw his way towards Kit. He was almost level with Kit when the shadow that had been hanging over them suddenly grew in size.

"Look out, Finn!" yelled Kit in terror.

An enormous airship had appeared from out of the clouds above them. Two dark spies were sitting under it, talking excitedly.

"The dark spies are controlling these creatures!" yelled Kit. "They are forcing them to come out in the daylight." He could see the spies were holding a metal device that crackled with an odd energy.

The creatures had increased their attack with the arrival of the dark spies. Wave after wave of

them surged towards the boys.

"Can you cover me, Finn?" begged Kit breathlessly.

Finn knew Kit must have a plan. He curled his cape around both of them, to protect them from the creatures. Behind him, Kit was using his climbing ax to chip away at the eyelid of the stone statue.

"I've got it!" he gasped. Finn saw a flash of orange light in Kit's hand – the amber jewel!

More creatures were appearing. "We need to attack that airship!" yelled Finn. "Throw your climbing hook at it, Kit. It might puncture it!"

Kit threw his climbing hook with all of his might, but it was no use. The hook just slid off the hot-air balloon above the airship. Things were looking desperate.

Suddenly, the creatures around Finn began to howl in pain. Pulses of light were attacking them from below. Finn peered down and saw Izzy. She was clambering up the stone face! She was using the metal device Maxine had given her to send bolts of light at the creatures!

Finn grinned. A crazy plan had come to him. He threw himself straight at one of the creatures, landing clumsily on its back. He was riding it!

"Aim that light at me," he yelled to Izzy.

Izzy aimed the light device towards the creature Finn was riding. She turned its power dial to maximum. They needed all its strength now. A

wave of energy burst from the machine. It pushed the creature upwards! It was heading straight for the hot-air balloon. Finn clung to its back with all of his might.

The creature's sharp claws scraped along the entire side of the balloon and punctured it. The airship plummeted swiftly downwards!

Chapter 6: A Fish out of Water

The energy from Izzy's light machine was fading. The creature holding Finn dropped suddenly in the air and Finn was thrown off its back. He landed heavily on the cliff next to Kit and Izzy, rubbing his elbow.

The three of them stood watching the airship spiral down through the clouds. They could hear the frustrated shrieking of the dark spies as they lost control of both their airship and the flying creatures. Within seconds, they had dropped down through the cloud and disappeared from sight.

The three friends found themselves surrounded by peaceful silence. The sharp-clawed creatures had lost all their malice now the dark spies weren't controlling them. A vast cloud of them flew harmlessly away.

Monk tugged at Izzy's coat. She looked down. He was holding the orb. He had gently taken it out of her pocket. It was time to resume

the quest and release the next Guardian! Kit
grinned at him and quickly rammed the amber
jewel into the orb.

A vivid golden light suddenly dazzled them.
Rubbing his eyes, Finn could just make out the
outline of the new Guardian against the sun.
The creature was floundering oddly. He landed
clumsily on the rock above them. Was he
wounded?

It soon became clear that the Guardian was not in its natural habitat. He flapped around on the rocks, gasping for breath. Long delicate fins, the color of rain, flapped powerlessly in the air.

"It's an Aquareon!" murmured Izzy. "I don't think he can breathe in the air up here."

The creature was desperate to leave the top of the mountain. His eyes throbbed wildly as he fought to breathe. He used his long tail to propel himself clumsily towards the edge of the stone face. He would soon be gone.

Finn was feeling very confident after his day of adventure in the clouds. "If the Aquareon can't survive up here, then we must all go back down to earth," he urged his friends. He climbed onto the Aquareon's back, making room for his friends behind him. Monk scampered up and buried himself in Finn's cloak.

"Monk has the right idea," said Izzy nervously. "I wish I could tie myself in somewhere safe for

this journey too!" Finn held onto her as she held
tightly onto the Aquareon.

The Aquareon threw himself off the top of the
mountain. His fins unfurled like wings, helping him
glide more gently. Within seconds, they had left
the huge stone face and the mountain behind them.

Finn was looking thoughtful. "The orb gave us no clues about where the jewel was this time. It's also the first time we escaped from difficulty without the Guardian's help," he told the others. "It was Izzy's light machine that got rid of those terrifying creatures and helped us burst the airship."

"It wasn't just me," said Izzy with a grin. "Kit's amazing climbing skills got us up to the amber jewel."

"I might be able to climb," added Kit, "but I would NEVER have thought of leaping onto a flying creature and using its claws as an arrow, like Finn did!"

It had indeed been an amazing day. They had rescued another Guardian and managed to escape from a sky full of winged enemies. Izzy looked down at the ground far below them. "I wonder where we're heading next?" she grinned.

Glossary

battered	– beat persistently or hard
crouched	– bent over, low to the ground
fled	– ran away from danger
grasping	– gripping firmly
habitat	– natural environment of a person or animal, place where it is most comfortable
horde	– a large group or crowd
hurled	– threw with great force
irritable	– easily annoyed, impatient
magnificent	– incredible and sublime
malice	– desire to inflict harm or injury on another
maximize	– give the greatest possible amount of something
microscopic	– so tiny it is invisible without the use of a microscope
minimal	– the least possible amount

miniscule	– very small
panted	– breathed hard and quickly
peered	– looked searchingly so as to see more clearly
propel	– make something move forward
snarling	– speaking or growling in a threatening manner
startling	– surprising
undergrowth	– bushes and small trees

Bounty in the Lagoon

Book 8

This book offers the reader the opportunity to read words with root words that relate to parts of the body and life, such as 'cap', 'man', 'spec' and 'viv'.

Contents

Chapter 1: Into the Blue

Racing down to earth on the back of an Aquareon was both exciting and terrifying. Monk peered out from inside Finn's coat. His eyes were wide with fear.

"Don't worry, Monk!" yelled Izzy. "I think we're nearly there."

They swooped down over a deep blue ocean. Finn scanned the horizon, then pointed excitedly. He had spotted land! The Guardian flew towards an amazing city, right on the edge of the coast. The buildings were bathed in golden sunlight.

"It looks like we're heading there!" said Kit.

Monk scampered across to Izzy and buried his face in her neck. Was he frightened? What had he seen? Izzy peered down at the beautiful city. "There's no one here," she told Finn. "It's completely deserted."

Finn looked down at the streets of domed buildings. They were all totally empty.

"Look at that!" yelled Kit. "There, by the harbor. It's a giant warrior!"

A huge warrior was straddling the harbor entrance. Sunlight sparkled off his rusted metal armor. The Aquareon suddenly swooped low over the city. He flew straight between the warrior's massive iron legs!

Izzy closed her eyes in terror. She was certain they were about to be captured! Suddenly

she heard Kit. He was laughing with relief.

"It's OK, Izzy. He won't harm us. It's an enormous statue!"

The Aquareon soared onwards, along the coastline. Before long, they had left the deserted city far behind them. They flew over lush tropical forest. Beneath them was a maze of rivers. Plants overhung the fast-flowing waterways. The Aquareon lurched suddenly in the air. He began to dive swiftly downwards, aiming straight at the water.

"Jump!" yelled Kit. He was just in time. The three friends managed to leap off the Aquareon's back just as he crashed into the water. By the time they resurfaced, he had disappeared.

Chapter 2: Emerald Forest

The three friends swam quickly to the riverbank. Monk clung to Finn's shoulder, chattering excitedly. They clambered out of the water and lay on the soft grass to rest.

"There are only three more Guardians left to find," said Izzy. She turned the amber necklace slowly in her hand, before tucking it back into her pocket.

Kit and Finn were busy studying the map. "I think I've worked out where we are," said Kit. He pointed to a maze of rivers on the map. "We're in a tropical forest. I think the next monument is around this next bend," he added, with sparkling eyes.

Izzy peered at the map. "It looks like another statue," she said.

They began to follow the twisted path of rivers, picking their way slowly through the exotic flowers and bushes that lined the riverbanks.

They had been walking for some time when they discovered the ruins of a small village.

"It looks as if it has been attacked," Izzy whispered sadly.

The village was totally devastated. Debris from shattered stone buildings surrounded the base of a broken statue. The trees and bushes around it were crushed and trampled.

"I've got a bad feeling about this," said Finn. "Where are all the people who lived here?"

The three friends began to look through the wreckage, searching for clues. Izzy bent down to read a small sign at the base of the broken statue.

"May the Merman return in our lifetime," she read slowly. "The Merman WAS our next monument and something has taken him," she speculated. A sudden shout startled Izzy. "I think there's someone here," she yelled. "They're trapped under these wooden slats!" Finn and Kit lifted the heavy slats. A small girl scrambled out from underneath them.

"My name is Shumi," she told them tearfully. "My father is Captain Pablo. We were fishing here when the kraken burst out of the water and trashed this place. It has taken the statue of the Merman with it!"

Izzy took Shumi's hand. "Let's see if we can find your father," she said gently.

Shumi led them quickly through the forest. She was excited to hear about their quest.

"I'm sure the next jewel will be hidden somewhere inside the Merman," she told them. "He has always stood guard over our village." She rubbed her face, with a puzzled expression. "The kraken has lived in an old sunken ship for years," she explained, "but it has never been to the village before. I don't understand why it would have suddenly decided to take the statue."

Chapter 3: Blind Vision

Finn and Kit exchanged worried glances, but said nothing. They both knew exactly who might be behind the kraken's sudden change of behavior. The dark spies!

They walked for a long time. There was no sign of Shumi's father. Suddenly Shumi let go of Izzy's hand. She ran towards a small waterfall. In front of it was her father, fishing.

Izzy noticed a scarf tied tightly round Pablo's eyes. Was he injured? Pablo turned when he heard his daughter's excited laugh. He hugged her close to him when he heard her story.

"Shumi is safe because of you," he told them gratefully as he waded across the stream towards them.

Pablo was not injured. He was blind. He explained why. "I know this kraken of old," he said fearfully. "It sank my ship, and it was in a battle with the kraken that I lost my sight!"

He listened thoughtfully as Finn told him about their quest.

"You must let me help you," he urged the three friends. "The kraken is a powerful beast. I doubt those dark spies would have been able to control it. I think it will have either smashed the Merman statue to pieces or swallowed him."

Izzy gasped with shock. "Eaten the monument?" she asked in horror. "What will happen to the amber Guardian if it has been swallowed?"

"The kraken has been using my old sunken ship as its lair for years," Pablo told them. "It has probably returned there. If we've any hope of finding your amber Guardian, it'll be there."

Kit looked around them. There was no sign of water deep enough to conceal a shipwreck. How would they find it?

Pablo tilted his head to one side, listening to the sounds around them. "My sight has gone, but I have fantastic hearing," he told them with a grin. "I can get you to the shipwreck with my ears." Holding Shumi's hand, he set off confidently upstream.

The three friends began to splash through the shallow water behind him. Finn swung Monk up onto his shoulder. "This time we have someone else to follow!" he told the monkey affectionately.

They emerged suddenly out of the forest and
into an idyllic lagoon. The water was a bright
turquoise color and was surrounded by flowers
of all colors. It was a beautiful sight. Kit gave
a whoop of excitement. In the middle of the
lagoon was Pablo's ship!

Chapter 4: Beneath the Wreck

Izzy felt a sudden prickle of fear. She peered behind her. She was sure she could hear rustling behind them. Was something, or someone, following them? It could be the dark spies.

"We need to be careful," she whispered to the others. She took hold of Shumi's hand and squeezed it. She didn't want to worry Shumi, but she had a strong feeling the dark spies were not far away.

Pablo pointed out to the lagoon. "If the statue of the Merman is still intact, he could be somewhere inside my ship."

Pablo and Shumi stayed at the edge of the forest. Shumi was keen to go out to the ship, but Izzy wanted to make sure she was safe. "Stay here, Shumi," she said gently. "We need someone on shore as a lookout."

Kit and Finn waded out towards the ship.
Izzy scanned the lagoon. Maybe there was
another way for her and Monk to reach the deck
of the ship. Monk had been through enough
adventures underwater.

Kit and Finn reached the shipwreck. They clambered up the old fishing ropes onto the deck. A heap of wooden slats lay at their feet. Kit tugged them to the edge of the ship and leaned them against the side. He had made a bridge between the ship and the shore!

Izzy and Monk clambered across the makeshift bridge. Monk was chattering excitedly. Izzy looked down at him affectionately. "You are nearly as good a climber as Kit," she said with a grin.

The four of them searched the deck quickly, but found nothing. "We need to look underwater," said Kit. "If the kraken has brought the statue of the Merman back here, it might have hidden him in its lair."

Izzy turned the orb around in her hands. She was hoping for a clue, but the orb was giving nothing away. She passed it to Finn.

"You stay on deck with Monk," she told him. "It's safest if we have two of us above and two of us below water." She and Kit exchanged grins and leaped into the lagoon.

Chapter 5: Dangerous Exploration

Reflected sunlight rippled underwater and helped them see their way. Izzy pointed to a jagged hole in the hull of the ship and the two of them swam steadily towards it.

They clambered into a room deep inside the hull. The floor was strewn with treasure! It was scattered in piles amid hunks of broken stone and rusted metalwork. Kit thought it looked exactly like the booty from a raid. He signaled to Izzy that they should search through it.

Luckily, part of the hull was still above water. They took it in turns to swim up and breathe gulps of fresh air. Sadly, their search of the hull was useless. There was no sign of the Merman statue.

They both swam up for air. "I'm going to explore further down," said Kit. "Maybe the statue is in one of the chambers deeper in the ship."

Izzy was going back to the surface to see if Pablo had any other ideas about where to search.

"Be careful," she told Kit with a shudder. "You don't want to be trapped too far down if that kraken comes back."

She clambered up through the wreck of the hull and into the sunlight. Finn and Monk were nowhere in sight. She shielded her eyes against the sun as she scanned the horizon. Where were they?

There was no sign of Finn or Monk anywhere. The lagoon was bathed in sunlight, but was eerily silent. Izzy whirled around. Shumi and Pablo had gone too. Where had everyone gone?

The cracked wooden floor of the deck suddenly began to tremble underneath Izzy's feet! She tried to steady herself, but it was no use. She was thrown backwards as a huge tidal force surged through the water beneath the ship!

Izzy caught a glimpse of two dark characters disappearing rapidly into the trees at the edge of the lagoon. The dark spies! They were behind this. Fear gripped her heart. Her friends were in danger. If something terrible was happening underwater, then they would need her help. She took a deep breath and dived into the lagoon.

Izzy soon found out what was causing the surge of energy through the water. The dark spies had summoned the kraken back to its lair! Its huge coiled tentacles circled the hull. It was squeezing hard. Izzy knew it would not take long for the wooden ship to be crushed into splinters.

The kraken's smaller tentacles were snaking their way through the water, exploring hungrily. Izzy looked for its head, then gasped with shock as she saw it emerge from under the hull. It was even more terrifying than she had imagined.

Chapter 6: Perilous Tentacles!

Izzy swam back to the surface, hungrily gasping for air. She needed time to make a plan. She stayed close to the hull of the ship, kicking her legs underwater to keep her afloat. She tried to draw a rough picture of the layout of the ship in her head. Where could Kit be hiding?

A sudden tug at her ankle left Izzy no time to make a plan. The kraken had found her! A tentacle wrapped around her leg and pulled hard. Izzy was yanked underwater! She tried to clutch hold of the ship, but the kraken was too strong for her. It pulled so hard that she crashed against the side of the ship.

The last thing Izzy felt was a sharp blow to the side of her head. She was unconscious when the kraken pulled her underwater. It was dragging her deep down under the ship.

Finn saw this happening, but couldn't stop it! He and Monk had climbed further down into the

ship and had discovered a watertight cabin.

He pressed his face against a glass porthole, desperate to see where the kraken was heading. He knew he had to think fast. Izzy would not survive long unconscious underwater. He clutched the orb tightly to his chest while he tried frantically to come up with a plan. Suddenly Finn caught a glimpse of something familiar! A faint amber light was glowing from the bottom of the lagoon!

Monk chattered with excitement as they peered through the murky glass of the porthole. Was the light coming from the amber jewel?

A sudden movement in the water caught Finn's eye. Kit was swimming hard, through the water, towards the amber light. The amber jewel was partially hidden in a heap of broken stone. It was the remains of the Merman statue. Kit scrabbled through the rubble and grabbed the gem.

Finn looked down at the orb in his hand. The amber jewel was no use without the orb. "It's time to go, Monk," Finn whispered urgently. He and Monk clambered upwards, out onto the deck. "Head for the shore, Monk," Finn told the little monkey. "Find Shumi and Pablo and keep them away from the water!" He gripped Monk's arm for a second, then turned and dived back into the lagoon.

Finn swam down towards Kit, holding the orb out in front of him. Kit turned towards him.

His huge grin was lit up by the amber jewel, now gripped in his hand! They began to swim towards each other.

The kraken's slippery tentacles snaked across the water towards Finn and Kit. They were closing in all around them. Eager tentacles began to curl around both boys. It was too late! They were going to be captured! A faint blue light was shining now from an opening in the orb. Finn and Kit locked eyes. They thrust their outstretched arms towards each other. Kit jammed the amber jewel into the orb!

Chapter 7: Silvery Savior

A mass of spiraling bubbles filled the water. It was enough to confuse the kraken for a second. Its grip on the boys loosened, giving them a chance to escape. The new Guardian was emerging from the amber jewel! At first it was hard to see anything clearly. Then the bubbles cleared slightly to reveal a powerful silvery being. It had the body of a man and the tail of a fish. The Merman!

The Merman launched an attack on the kraken! He chased after it as it retreated deeper into the water.

Kit and Finn were almost out of air. They swam to the surface and quickly gasped fresh air into their aching lungs. Beneath them an epic battle was taking place. The silvery Guardian raced through the water, forcing the kraken deep down into the depths of the lagoon.

Kit and Finn watched the last tentacles of the kraken disappear into the depths. A terrified shrieking from Monk made them look up. Something had just floated to the surface of the lagoon. It was Izzy! She was not moving. The boys swam across to her, desperately hoping she was still alive.

Finn's eyes were red with hot tears as he strode out of the lagoon. He was carrying Izzy's limp body in his arms. They were too late!

Shumi splashed out towards them. She placed her warm hands on Izzy's forehead. Izzy shuddered and opened her eyes. "She's still alive!" whooped Kit with relief.

It was getting late. Everyone had their part of the tale to tell. Only Izzy noticed the Merman Guardian leap out of the sea. He hovered proudly against the backdrop of the setting sun.

Glossary

amid	– in the middle of
booty	– something that is taken by robbery
conceal	– hide, keep out of sight
debris	– remains of something broken or destroyed
glimpse	– very brief look
hull	– lower part of a ship
intact	– not damaged; whole, complete
jagged	– with rough points or edges
lagoon	– pool of shallow water seeped from the sea
limp	– lacking any energy or strength
merman	– mythological creature with the head and body of a man and the tail of a fish
porthole	– round watertight window in the side of a ship

resurfaced – came back to the surface again

rubble – broken pieces of something that has been destroyed

speculated – thought or had a theory about something

straddling – standing with legs wide apart, one on either side of something

strode – walked powerfully with long steps

summoned – called to action or commanded

thrust – pushed or shoved, with force

turquoise – a greenish-blue color

unfurled – spread or shook out

watertight – designed so that water can't get into or through it

wreckage – remains of something that has been wrecked or broken

Sounds of the Sirens

The City of Epicantor

TITAN STRAITS

STRATOS MOUNTAINS

LUCA JUNGLE

ARON STEPPES

EMERALD FALLS

The City of Athelos

WASTELAND WILDERNESS

BITTERBOON MOUNTAINS

Book 9

This book offers the reader the opportunity to read words with root words that relate to memory, such as 'mem'.

Contents

Chapter 1: A Familiar Landmark

The Merman left without even speaking to them. Finn and Kit exchanged grins. "I think we're on our own with finding the next monument!" said Kit.

It had been a long day. They were all close to exhaustion. Pablo helped them create a makeshift shelter at the edge of the beach. "Night is coming," he told them. "Sleep now and recover your strength. I have a feeling you will need all your energy tomorrow."

The next morning was bright and sunny. Shumi and Monk were playing chase. Pablo listened to them playing, a wistful look on his face. "It is great to hear Shumi laugh," he told Izzy. "Sometimes it can be lonely for her here."

Finn was studying the map. "I know why the Guardian left us here!" he said in excitement. "The next monument is back in the town with the huge statue we flew under, on the way here!"

"That's the Port of Yaneth," said Pablo. "The quickest way back there is by boat. Let me help you make a coracle."

Pablo explained that a coracle was a small boat – similar in shape to half a walnut shell. The three friends collected armfuls of bamboo. Pablo showed them how to weave the strips into a watertight boat.

By midday, they had a boat that could take them back upriver to the sea and the Port of Yaneth.

"Where's Monk?" asked Finn as they prepared to set sail.

Shumi was standing by the boat. Monk was close at her side. "I think Monk may be needed here, Finn," said Izzy softly.

Finn's heart sank. The little monkey had been through so many adventures with them. Had he decided to stay here? "You have helped us so much," he told Monk. "Our quest is nearly over. You must feel free to choose what you do next."

Monk gave Finn a quick hug. He turned to hold Shumi's hand. He had made his choice.

Pablo handed Izzy a conch shell.

"Keep this somewhere safe," he told her. "Blow into it if you find yourself in trouble. Remember, music can be a powerful weapon."

Izzy was puzzled. Surely music could only ever be used for good? She thanked Pablo and tucked the shell safely into a deep pocket. This quest had taught her never to ignore good advice.

Chapter 2: Perilous Waters

Finn took one last look back at Shumi and Monk as they set sail. He could hear Shumi's laughter. Monk had made the right decision.

They rowed swiftly upriver and out into the open sea. The sunny sky slowly darkened and a cold wind began to blow. "I think a storm is coming!" yelled Izzy.

Waves began to crash against the side of the tiny coracle. "There's too much water in the bottom of the boat!" said Finn grimly. He stood up shakily, trying to scoop up water with his hands. A sudden huge wave knocked him overboard!

Izzy saw Finn disappear under the frothing water. He rose to the surface again, but the current was very strong. Within seconds he was a long way behind the boat. "Finn!" she screamed in terror.

The boat was now crashing through a series of sharp rocks. Kit grabbed his rope. He threw a

hooped ring of rope at a jutting rock. It caught
and held firm. "Help me pull on it, Iz!" yelled Kit.
"We need to get closer to Finn."

Finn could see Izzy and Kit tugging frantically
on the rope to pull the boat closer to him. He
tried to swim in their direction.

This time, Kit unhooked the rope from the
rocks. He threw it towards Finn. Finn saw the
rope snaking through the sky above him, but he
couldn't swim close enough to catch it.

"Again!" yelled Izzy. She yanked the rope out of the water and hurled it out again. Finn just managed to catch it. He hung onto it with all of his might as Kit rowed the coracle closer to him. Kit and Izzy were just able to drag Finn's battered body back into the boat. He was safe!

The storm was at last dying down when a dark shadow loomed over them. Izzy looked up fearfully. She grinned. It was good news for once! Their tiny boat was sailing right between the legs of the almighty statue of Yaneth.

The three of them gazed up at the statue in awe. It was much more detailed than they had first thought. The statue was formed of metal plates, secured with small screws. It had been badly damaged by the wild winds sweeping in from the sea. In some places, the panels had come loose or fallen away.

"He's still incredible," breathed Izzy.

Their little boat sailed under the statue's

massive legs and bobbed into the harbor. The city seemed intact, but was completely abandoned.

Izzy had a sudden jolt of memory as she looked at some of the buildings. "I have heard my father describe this place," she whispered nervously. "This town was taken over by evil spirits. It is said they were the ghostly foot soldiers of the dark sorcerer." She gave a sudden shudder as if cold. "They feed on human fear."

Chapter 3: I Spy an Amber Jewel

They left the boat and began to explore the deserted city. At first they walked nervously, jumping at any movement. Gradually they relaxed. It really did seem as if the place was totally deserted. Maybe even the ghostly spirits had moved on?

Kit suddenly let out a cry of excitement. He ran towards a strange mechanical device. He began to turn an assortment of lenses and gears that hung from it.

"Come and see, Izzy!" he yelled. He tilted the device upwards and peered into it. "Look through this!"

Izzy looked through the device. "Kit!" she screamed. "The statue of Yaneth is moving! It's getting closer!"

Kit laughed. "It's OK, Izzy. The statue's not moving. There's a magnifying glass inside that device that makes it seem much closer." Izzy peered through the glass again. She could see

Yaneth's helmet, as clearly as if it was next to her.

"Kit!" she gasped. "I can see the next amber jewel. It's embedded in the statue's helmet!"

The three of them began to run towards the statue. A wailing siren song suddenly came from nowhere. The air was filled with it. Instinctively, Finn covered his ears with his hands. Izzy and Kit were already under the spell of the music. They began to drift silently away, following the sound of the music. Finn followed them, keeping to the shadows. He needed to find out what was calling them.

Finn followed Izzy and Kit up some stairs
into a shadowy courtyard. He gasped in horror.
Flying above his head were three enormously tall
women. They had huge feathery wings sprouting
from their backs. Their huge wings began to
beat with excitement as they spotted Kit and Izzy

drifting silently towards them.

Finn shuddered. He remembered Izzy talking about these creatures. They were the viron. They hypnotized people with their siren song. As he watched, another character stepped out of an archway and joined the viron. It was one of the dark spies!

Finn needed to rescue his friends. He had to create a noise strong enough to drown out the siren song. At the top of the steps was a ceremonial gong. It was exactly what he needed! He ran forward, grabbing the drum stick from the ground beneath the gong. He began to beat out a loud, repetitive rhythm.

The powerful sound echoed from the gong. It was loud enough to break the viron's spell!

Izzy and Kit rubbed their eyes as if they were waking up after a deep sleep. They staggered around, trying to work out where they were.

Izzy was the first to work out what was happening. She pulled on Kit's arm and pointed towards Finn.

Finn was still beating out an insistent rhythm on the gong. "Run towards the statue, Izzy!" he yelled. He dropped the drum stick and ran to follow them.

The three of them stuck to the shadows as they ran, trying to make as little noise as possible. They didn't want the viron to catch them.

The statue of Yaneth had his feet firmly placed on the ground. The heels of his giant feet had doors in them! Inside was a steep metal staircase.

"Let's climb up inside," gasped Kit. "Maybe we can get as high as the amber jewel."

The three of them clambered higher and higher up inside the statue. Finn glanced behind them, relieved that the viron did not seem to be following them. He turned back when he heard Izzy gasp with shock.

The metal panels on the statue's chest had
been ripped apart by the weather. The metal
staircase had been destroyed. There was no other
route up the statue. The friends were stranded!

The wind was howling around them now.
"I've got more bad news," shouted Kit. He pointed
down to the base of the statue at a flurry of
shadowy figures. "The viron have found us!"

Chapter 4: Brave Inspirations

They needed to act fast. It wouldn't take the viron long to reach them. Izzy peered upwards, trying to find a way past the huge hole in the statue's chest. They needed to get that jewel.

"There are masses of tiny holes and scars in the metal," she told Kit. "Do you think you could get your grapple into some of them?"

A challenge like that was music to Kit's ears! He grinned broadly. "Great idea, Iz!" he said. He reached for his grapple and rope.

Kit threw his grapple up at the statue's chest. It caught in one of the deeper holes. He tugged the rope hard. It held strong. Izzy gritted her teeth. This was no time for a fear of heights. She knew she needed to muster all her courage.

The three of them ventured bravely out onto the statue's chest, clinging onto the ropes. Izzy gasped as the wind began to batter them from all sides.

Kit was the most nimble. He soon managed to scramble as high as Yaneth's shoulder. Izzy struggled to keep pace with the others. She was finding the climb both tough and frightening.

"Nearly there, Izzy!" yelled Finn, against the wind. He reached down to help pull her up.

A sudden burst of music caught them by surprise. Izzy turned her head to listen to it. She found herself staring straight into a mass of gray feathery wings. The viron were closing in on them!

"Finn!" she screamed desperately. "I'm losing my grip!" She began to slide rapidly back down the statue's massive torso!

Finn just managed to save her. He caught her arm and held tight. Izzy fumbled for a holding hole on the statue's chest. She began to inch her way back upwards.

Kit covered his ears with his hands. "Block out the music!" he yelled down to them. Izzy covered her ears, but Finn was struggling to regain his balance. Kit could see he was slowly falling under the music's hypnotic spell. His eyes were already misting over. They were losing him.

Suddenly Izzy remembered something Pablo had told her. "Music is a powerful weapon!" she yelled. She tugged the giant shell Pablo had given her out

of her pocket. Bringing it up to her lips, she blew into it with all her strength.

A deep, sad sound poured out of the shell. It echoed around them. Izzy blew again and again, harder and harder, using the music like a wall of sound. She was trying to drown out the sound of the viron's music. Gradually it began to work!

Finn shook his head and his eyes cleared. The spell was broken! He began to scramble up the statue behind Izzy.

Chapter 5: Sound it Out!

Izzy carried on blowing as hard as she could into the shell. Finn began to beat on the metal panels of Yaneth's chest with his fists. Between them they made a huge amount of noise.

The viron screeched in frustration. They twisted their heads from side to side, trying to avoid the sound. Their huge great wings began to lose their power as they struggled unsteadily to keep aloft.

Kit saw his chance while the viron were distracted. He swung his grapple up towards the statue's mighty head. It caught firm. He began to climb nimbly up the rope. The next amber jewel was in sight!

Kit scrambled across the head of the statue. The amber jewel was lodged in Yaneth's helmet, just as they had seen from the ground. Kit ran his fingers over the gem. Perhaps the next Guardian was going to be a great warrior?

Kit peered into the face of the statue. "I hope you can help us find a safe way out of this mess," he muttered. He swung his grapple at the amber jewel. It was time to release the next Guardian.

Below him, Finn and Izzy were getting tired. More and more viron were appearing. Swarms of them circled in the air, ready to attack. Their eerie singing was beginning to drown out the noise that two exhausted humans could make.

"Drop the shell, Izzy!" yelled Finn. "Put your hands over your ears! It's our only hope of escaping that singing."

Izzy squinted up at the enormous head of the statue. Had Kit reached the amber jewel yet? She knew their only real hope would be if they could release the Guardian.

Kit's grinning face suddenly appeared high above her. He was leaning out, away from the statue, holding something in his hand. "Get ready to catch!" he shouted.

Izzy leaned out as far as she could. She didn't look down. Kit must be holding the amber jewel in his hand! She stretched up, just as he dropped it. She caught it!

Izzy rammed the amber jewel into the orb. It was time for it to release its prisoner.

The next Guardian appeared in a powerful rush of air and light. The three friends were hurled back by the force of the blast. They grabbed for handholds on the metal of the statue. Yaneth himself was trembling now with vibrations from the force of the explosion.

Chapter 6: A Favor from Fae

It was difficult to see exactly what happened to the viron. The wind had whipped everything into a frenzy. The burst of light was so powerful that it was hard to see. When the wind dropped, the viron were gone. Only a few stray feathers remained, drifting in the breeze.

Kit pointed down, way below them, at the choppy sea in the harbor. They could just make out the bony figures of the viron tumbling into the water.

The Guardian began to take shape. She was an elegant figure, more human-looking than any of the previous Guardians. She smiled broadly at them. As the three friends gazed on, entranced, the Guardian cupped her hands to her mouth and sang a musical thanks.

"You have released me at an important moment in history," she told them. "My name is Fae. It is time for me to join the other Guardians. We must put an end to the deadly threat that the

sorcerer presents to our world. Without your help I would have remained trapped on Yaneth forever."

Izzy was holding very tightly to the statue behind her. She felt dizzy and light-headed. She knew things would get worse if she looked down. She did not let her eyes leave Fae's face. "Fae," she said softly, "I need help."

Finn took one glance at Izzy and knew there was not a moment to lose. If they stayed where they were much longer, Izzy's fear of heights would be too great for her to control.

"Can you help us get back down to the ground?" Finn begged Fae. "I don't think Izzy can make the climb."

Fae raised her arms slowly upwards. Izzy floated away from the statue and up into the air! Both she and Fae were floating in the breeze!

Izzy gasped in shock, then grinned as she realized she was floating and not falling. Seconds later, Kit and Finn floated up to join them in mid-air!

The four of them drifted slowly back down to the harbor, supported on a gentle current of warm air. It was an experience none of them would ever forget. They were almost sad to reach firm ground again. "I wish I could keep that power!" said Kit with a grin.

Fae's next words brought them quickly back to reality.

"There is a great conflict ahead," she told them. "We must all prepare for it. The Guardians are a mighty force, but you three are also going to have a huge part to play. The sorcerer has stolen three things from the Guardians. We will need to retrieve them. Their powers will be the vital key in the final battle."

Fae rose again, into the air just above the harbor. "We will meet again very soon," she called down to them. "Stay strong, my friends, and be ready. The time for the final conflict is very close now."

The three friends bid her a warm farewell before sitting down on the harbor wall to gather their strength. Finn looked at Kit and could see the excitement in his friend's eyes. He saw the strength in Izzy as she breathed deeply, calming herself for the next part of their quest. He had a tight feeling in his chest. It was time to be strong. The battle was coming.

Glossary

assortment – mixture

batter – damage by beating or hitting hard

conflict – fight or battle

describe – talk or write about something

eerie – creepy or unnerving

frenzy – wild excitement or agitation

frothing – foaming or bubbling due to rapid movement

jutting – sticking up

makeshift – something temporary made to solve a problem in an emergency

muster – gather up or summon

retrieve – bring something back to its former place

staggered – walked unsteadily

stranded – left in a helpless position

swiftly – very quickly

torso – trunk of the human body

ventured	– braved the dangers of something
vital	– of life or death importance
wistful	– filled with longing or yearning

Guardians Unite

Book 10

This book offers the reader the opportunity to read words with root words that relate to actions, such as 'ject', 'tract', 'struct', 'labor', 'fact' and 'form'.

Contents

Chapter 1: A Light in the Darkness

The three friends had no trouble finding a warm, dry place to spend the night in the deserted city. They were woken from a deep sleep by a bright light shining from the orb. It projected the shape of a tall, twisted needle onto a wall next to them. Izzy shuddered. "That clue is easy to read," she said nervously. "It's the sorcerer's tower. I've seen it on the map."

They studied the map closely to work out the route. "It's a tricky journey," said Finn slowly. "The first part of it is by sea. It's lucky we kept our coracle."

They collected a few basic resources from some of the deserted buildings around them. Kit found a sack of nuts and dried fruit for a quick meal. "I'm looking forward to having some hot food again once this quest is over," he joked.

Finn grinned in response, but he could not shake off the feeling of tightness in his chest. There was space for one last amber jewel on the necklace. They needed to find it, release the last Guardian, and face the final battle. He hoped with all his heart that they were strong enough.

They set off once more for the open sea. Finn labored to steer the tiny boat towards a rocky formation just visible on the horizon.

It was a tough journey. Time and time again, waves crashed over the top of the makeshift boat and drenched them. They worked as a team, using their hands to scoop water out of the boat.

The wild journey had injected Kit with a new surge of energy. He loved the excitement of being constantly in motion. "This boat has been fantastic, hasn't it, Izzy?" he yelled, as yet another wave of icy water crashed into them.

Izzy was less enthusiastic. "I'm planning on staying on dry land for as long as possible once this quest is over," she told Kit firmly.

At last, the sea calmed and the coastline came into view. Izzy smiled in relief.

They left the coracle tied to a rock near the edge of the sea and set off across a vast golden beach. It was a scorching hot day and the sun beat down on them relentlessly. They trudged onwards, heading for the rocks on the distant horizon. At last, the light began to fade, taking the heat of the sun with it.

The three exhausted friends stopped to rest, slumped against each other on the sand.

Finn was anxious to keep moving. "We need to reach that cluster of rocks before nightfall," he urged the others. "We have no protection out here. We are a sitting target."

The sun was setting by the time they reached the rocks. "These rocks look like sharp teeth," shuddered Izzy. "I don't think they were arranged as a welcome."

Finn was as nervous as she was. He had hoped the rocks would offer them shelter, but it felt almost as if they had walked into a trap.

Kit pointed to a tall twisting tower beyond the rocks. "I think we may have reached our destination," he said quietly.

It was the first time Finn had seen fear in his friend's eyes. "Stay strong, Kit," he urged him. "We would never have got this far without your bravery."

They were interrupted by a sudden gasp from Izzy. "There's someone out there!" she hissed. "I saw movement."

The three of them crouched down in the sand. Sudden flickers of light lit up the rocks ahead of them. A grumbling character stumbled into view. A dark spy! One by one, a crowd of dark spies

emerged from behind the rocks. They carried lit torches to help them see in the dark. Izzy found the sight of so many of them terrifying. She forced herself to stay quiet and still.

The dark spies did not see them. They were looking towards the tower. One of them pointed towards it as he talked. It was obvious they were heading there too.

"It's getting dark now," whispered Izzy. "We have no torches. How will we reach the tower before they do?"

Chapter 3: Infiltrate the Base

Kit reached into his pocket and carefully he pulled out a strange pair of goggles. "I found them in the deserted city," he whispered. Even in the fading light, they could see at once what made the goggles so unusual. The glass lenses were a deep red color!

Kit tugged the goggles over his head and settled them on his eyes. He looked like some strange form of insect! He stood up and gazed ahead of him at the rocky terrain between him and the tower. Izzy gasped as she saw him weave a pathway between the rocks. The goggles were helping him see in the dark!

Kit scampered back to join them, breathless with excitement. The thought of outwitting the dark spies by racing them to the tower had really lifted his mood.

"Follow me closely, Izzy," he said. "If we stick together, we'll avoid any problems."

They set off across the rocky plain. Even with the goggles, it was a long, difficult journey in the dark. Gradually, they drew nearer and nearer to the menacing-looking tower.

Suddenly, they were startled by the sound of angry voices, very close at hand. The dark spies had stopped moving. The dark spies had set up camp for the night in a sandy hollow surrounded by tall rocks. Kit tugged on Izzy's arm, pulling her back into the shadows.

The sprawling camp completely blocked their route. There was no other option but to wait until the dark spies started moving again.

"Another obstruction!" hissed Kit in frustration. "We're losing time. We need to be ahead of the dark spies, not behind them."

Finn was distracted by a shadowy movement behind them. A soft thud confirmed his suspicions. Something heavy had just landed silently, very close to them. "Stay close," he whispered to Izzy. "Something is wrong here."

The shadows behind Finn rippled again and something stepped out in front of them. Izzy gave a gasp of delight. It was the Griffin!

The Griffin spoke quickly, in a hushed tone. "The Guardians are gathering. They are close to the tower and ready for the final battle," he said.

"We're ready to help," said Kit.

"The sorcerer has stolen three artefacts from the Guardians," the Griffin reminded them.

Kit's eyes lit up immediately. "Tell us more!" he said quickly.

"He has stolen Refolia's cloak of vines, the Quadrator's bow of light and the Merman's silver shield," said the Griffin. "These three things have great powers. Can you help us retrieve them?"

Kit already had a plan. He clambered onto the Griffin's back. "Climb aboard," he urged the others. "We need to get to the tower. We can't walk through the spies' camp but, with your help, Griffin, we can fly over it!"

Chapter 4: Towering Assault

The Griffin flew them swiftly through the dark sky, over the heads of the sleeping spies. He landed at the gateway to the sorcerer's tower. It was now the middle of the night. The silhouette of the tower loomed over them, dark and silent.

"We will meet again at dawn," said the Griffin. "You will need to search the tower for the stolen artefacts. The sorcerer will have them well guarded."

Finn had spotted a doorway at the base of the tower. "I don't think this doorway is guarded," he said. "It looks like our best chance of getting in."

Kit tried the door, but it was stuck fast. "Not necessarily a problem," he told Finn with a grin. He lodged his grapple in the keyhole of the door and began to wiggle it gently. Within seconds, he had managed to pick the lock!

Izzy grinned at him. "At last I am beginning to come round to your climbing skills!" she joked.

They were almost through the doorway
when a massive winged creature landed behind
them. Its huge wings knocked Finn to the ground.
"One of the stone sentries has come to life!" Finn
gasped. "We need to get inside that tower. RUN!"

The sentry was ready to attack. Finn was
aware of a sudden flash of white. What was it?
Had another sentry come to life?

It was not another sentry. The movement was the Unicorn they had once released from a fountain! The horned Guardian raised his mighty front legs and crashed them against the sentry's back. The sentry fell to the ground, winded. By the time it had staggered to its feet, Finn had joined his friends inside the safety of the tower.

Izzy was shaking with relief. "Once again the Unicorn has silently saved us," she said softly.

Finn barely heard her. He was peering into the shadowy hallway of the tower. Where would the sorcerer have hidden the stolen artefacts?

It was very hard to see. Izzy held up the orb, willing it to help them. To her surprise, a jet of white light shone from it. Was the orb trying to show them the way?

They followed the flickering light upwards, climbing higher and higher into the twisting tower. Their route was complex and heavily guarded. Time and time again, they had to duck into the

shadows to avoid the winged sentries.

Dawn was rising when they reached a balcony, way up on the outside of the tower.

"The staircase is broken here. We'll have to climb this next bit," said Finn.

A swarm of winged sentries suddenly spotted them. Within seconds, they were surrounded by a sea of snarling faces as the sentries flew up towards them. "What business have you here?" demanded the closest.

Chapter 5: Artefact Guardians

Finn was wracking his brains for an answer. Suddenly, something crashed heavily into the side of the sentry. It was Ignia! The mighty firebird beckoned to them to climb onto her back.

"There is no time to lose," she urged. "The artefacts are in a locked chamber, high up in the tower. Hold on tight and I'll fly you there." Her powerful wings knocked the sentries aside as she surged upwards, heading for the top of the tower.

Finn pointed down below them. The tower was completely surrounded now by a massive crowd of dark spies. There was movement at the edges of the crowd. A battle was already starting. The Guardians had arrived.

Kit was still looking at the top of the tower. "I can see the chamber!" he yelled. "It's got a metal gate protecting it, but I have an idea."

Kit yelled an urgent plan to Ignia. Hanging on to the giant bird with one arm, he stretched

across to the metal gate. He looped his strongest
climbing rope through it.

"Hold on tight!" yelled Izzy as Iginia swooped in
and grabbed both ends of the rope in her claws.
She flew backwards, tearing the metal gate out of
the stone wall of the tower. The chamber was open!

Kit had been clinging on to the side of the wall. He scrambled inside the chamber and retrieved the three artefacts the sorcerer had stolen. "We will need these," he said grimly. He threw the bow of light to Izzy. He tucked the vine cloak into his belt and handed the silver shield to Finn. Their battle was getting closer.

A group of dark spies had seen the three friends. They were in hot pursuit, swarming up the stairs towards the top of the tower.

The three of them ducked into an alcove, listening fearfully to the thundering feet of the dark spies as they drew nearer. There was

nowhere left to hide. Izzy peered down in terror.
"We still need to find the last amber jewel,"
whispered Izzy. "Do you have a plan, Finn?"

Finn grabbed the vine cloak from Kit's belt
and wrapped it tightly around the three of them.
Immediately they were invisible!

Safe inside the cloak of invisibility, the three
friends managed to reach the final room, high up
at the very top of the tower. Finn handed the
cloak back to Kit. "I have a feeling we're going
to meet the sorcerer very soon," he said. "We
will need to be able to see each other."

Chapter 6: Power of the Guardians

A door at the back of the hall suddenly burst open and three massive dark spies crashed into the room. "The sorcerer's bodyguards," whispered Finn. "Take care, Kit. These three are likely to have been chosen for their physical strength."

The spy nearest them leered maliciously. "Good-bye, small children," he mocked, as he held up a strange metal object. A terrifying red light shot from it, hot as fire and hissing like molten lava.

Finn thrust the silver shield up into the air, creating a barrier against the red light.

Kit and Izzy ducked quickly behind him. The red hot light hit the silver shield, but it could not pass through it! The power of the shield was too strong for the dark spies!

Aware of a commotion, a crowd of dark spies was now pouring into the chamber. Several of them cackled with joy at seeing all three friends together.

Izzy had a sudden wild fear that all was lost. The shield could not last long against such a force. She looked at the bow in her hand. Did it hold a power that could save them? She raised a trembling arm and aimed. An arrow shot up into the air and over the heads of the cackling band of dark spies.

A blaze of light followed the arrow, spreading through the room as quickly as spilled water. It hovered above the heads of the army of dark spies. Izzy saw the ones closest to her begin to rub their eyes. Was the bow of light sending them to sleep?

The light was indeed sending the spies to sleep. As it did so, it gently robbed them of the evil spell the sorcerer had woven over them. Izzy saw their faces relax. All malice gently left them. They were no longer the enemy!

Kit grinned, but his relief was short-lived. A terrifying figure strode through the doorway, his hooded eyes glinting with rage. The sorcerer had arrived.

The sorcerer's voice rippled with scorn. "You three children will never defeat me! I will never hand over all my power to you," he snarled. He raised his hand and sent a torrent of energy crackling through the air towards them. Finn just managed to lift his shield in time. The energy struck the shield, but could not pass through it.

"Use the bow of light, Izzy," he gasped. "That might destroy the sorcerer's negative energy! It's our only chance."

Bravely, Izzy stepped out from behind the protection of the silver shield. She raised her bow, and shot an arrow straight at the sorcerer. It bounced off him, leaving him completely unhurt. "His powers are too strong," yelled Izzy. "We can't defeat him!"

Finn spotted an enormous necklace swinging round the sorcerer's neck. It had been carefully manufactured to hold a huge glowing jewel. The last amber jewel!

"Aim an arrow at the amber jewel, Izzy!" he screamed. "Release the last Guardian!"

Izzy aimed, and shot an arrow straight at the heart of the amber jewel. It exploded in a blaze of light. The impact released the last Guardian. The sorcerer, robbed of all power now, cowered in the center of the ruined room.

Chapter 7: Freedom and Farewells

The last Guardian stepped into the light. "I am Ambevar," he told them warmly, "the last of the Guardians. Look outside. The other Guardians have been able to defeat the dark spies surrounding the tower."

Izzy raced to the window. It was true the battle had been won! The last few dark spies were running into the hills. The Guardians were cheering in triumph!

Within minutes, the victorious Guardians had gathered in the sorcerer's ruined chamber. Instinct made Izzy reach into her pocket and give Ambevar the orb. "The three of you have shown strength and great courage," said Ambevar. "You are a fantastic team."

Ambevar held the orb high up in the air. A bolt of light shot from it, aiming straight at the cowering sorcerer. The magical energy lifted the sorcerer up from the ground.

"No!" he screamed in rage. But it was no good. Within seconds, he had been absorbed into the dark center of the orb.

"He'll be out of everyone's way inside there," said Ambevar. A well of kindness opened up in his eyes as he looked at the three friends.

"The Guardians are now all freed. We owe you three our lives. We can return now to guarding the safety of both our worlds."

Saying good-bye to the ten Guardians was very emotional. "We will never forget you or this quest," Izzy told the Griffin tearfully.

It was time to return the artefacts to their rightful owners. Izzy could see the sadness in Kit's eyes as they handed them all back.

"Cheer up, Kit," she whispered with a smile. "The Griffin says we can keep the amber necklace. Finn's mom will get her birthday present after all!"

Kit laughed until tears ran from his eyes. It seemed as if a whole lifetime had passed since the three of them had met up in the marketplace.

"Show me the map, Finn," he said, his eyes twinkling. "I'll race you two back home."

Glossary

cackling – laughing in a shrill, broken way

commotion – violent or noisy disturbance

cowered – crouched with fear or shame

injected – introduced or added in something new or different

labored – worked hard

malice – evil intent

menacing – threatening to cause evil or harm

projected – threw or shone something upon a surface

relentlessly – without stopping

scampered – ran about playfully, like a child

scorching – burning, very hot

slumped – collapsed heavily

victorious – having won, achieved a victory

City of Secrets

Book 1

This book offers the reader the opportunity to read words with the suffixes s, es, ed and ing.

Contents

Chapter 1: Trouble at the Market

"Finn!" An excited cry rang out across the noisy hum of the bazaar. "I knew it was you, as soon as I spotted that cloak. I'm sure you've been wearing it since you were thirteen!"

Finn had been browsing the stalls for a gift for his mother. "Izzy!" he said in surprise. A tall girl with blonde spiky hair and a wide grin appeared. He hugged her warmly. "I thought you were still traveling?"

"I was," grinned Izzy, tapping a leather pouch in her pocket. "And we found some fantastic new healing herbs." Izzy was often away with her dad, collecting rare plant samples.

She pointed down at a pair of feet sticking out from under a stall next to them. "We got back late last night. Kit already has me out tracking down climbing hooks!"

A boy with round glasses and a lively face emerged from under the stall beside Izzy.

He was busy inspecting a handful of rusty hooks he had found under the stall.

"Great. I knew I'd find good ones here," he mumbled.

"Finn!" smiled Kit, as he looked up. "It's surprising to see you on dry land! Where's Korus?"

Finn, a fisherman, had met a talking songbird called Korus during an epic adventure at sea.

"Korus? He's flown south for the winter," answered Finn.

Just then a crowd of people began to push past them. "Stop that thief!" bellowed a sudden loud voice. "Grab him! Don't let him get away!"

A tiny barrel of fur shot out of the crowd of bodies and hurled itself into Finn's arms. Finn looked affectionately at the tiny monkey, now clinging to him. He rolled his eyes.

"Monk! What have you been up to now?" Monk thrust a metal chain into Finn's hand. He clung to Finn's chest. His tiny blue eyes were

wide with fear.

"I said grab him!" yelled an angry stall keeper. He pushed his way through the crowd towards them. He pointed angrily at Monk. "He's a thief!" he spat. "You need to pay for what he has stolen!"

"I'm so sorry, sir," apologized Finn. "He's a monkey. He doesn't understand he can't just pick things up if they don't belong to him." He looked at the man respectfully. "Please, whatever it is, let me pay for it, sir," he begged.

Izzy was hiding a smile. "I see Monk is up to his old tricks," she whispered to Kit, as Finn pleaded with the irate stall keeper.

Kit grinned and began searching through his pockets for cash. "Can we pay for it, sir?" he echoed. He held out a handful of battered notes.

They had just enough cash to calm down the angry stall keeper. "Keep him at home next time!" he snarled as he left. "In a cage if you have one!"

Finn had found Monk washed up on a beach, half-starved and with a badly injured leg. Nobody knew Monk's past. Finn had nursed him back to health and the two were now inseparable.

"You are a disaster, Monk," said Finn, with a grin. He rubbed the tiny monkey's chin affectionately.

"What did Monk pick up from that stand?" asked Izzy curiously. "Hopefully something you can give your mom for her birthday!"

Finn pulled the strange-looking necklace out of his pouch.

"Wow, it's lovely," gasped Izzy. She reached forward to pick it up. The battered necklace was very old and badly damaged. Most of its original jewels were missing.

"Lovely junk," snorted Kit. "Think how many climbing hooks we could have bought with all that cash. Finn's mom will just throw it away." He glanced at the necklace dismissively. "It only has one jewel left in it."

Izzy gazed at the necklace. A spidery metal clasp held the one large remaining jewel. She rubbed the dust off it with her fingers. It glowed with a soft orange light.

"You're wrong, Kit," she said, her eyes sparkling with excitement. "This looks like real amber!"

Sunlight lit up the amber jewel, picking out the shadows deep inside it. Izzy stared at the beautiful stone. It was odd. It almost looked as if something inside it was moving.

All of a sudden, Finn felt uneasy. Cold prickles of fear made him shudder. He had a strong feeling that they were being observed. From the corner of his eye he saw a figure slipping silently away into the shadows. Had someone been watching them? Were they looking for the necklace? Or was it just his own fear playing tricks on him?

"It's time to move on," he told the others. "I have a feeling there may be more to this necklace than we think."

Izzy hadn't seen the shadowy figure watching them. She was still excited about the necklace. "Do you think it could be lost treasure?" she asked. Her eyes glinted hopefully.

"If it is, then it's been lost for a long time!" laughed Kit. "It looks as if it's been at the bottom of the sea for about a hundred years!"

"I know someone who can value it," said Izzy. "A shopkeeper my dad has talked about."

"Worth a try, I guess," shrugged Kit. He was busy hanging his new climbing hooks onto his belt.

There was no sign now of anyone watching them. Finn began to relax. The necklace was just a broken tangle of metal from a junk stall. No one would be looking for it.

They strolled through the market to the tiny shop Izzy had spoken about. They pushed their way through a heavy velvet curtain. The darkened room was filled with piles of strange twisted metal.

"Now, this IS treasure," breathed Kit as they gazed around them. The room smelled of moldy paper, damp and decay. A flickering light came from candles, half hidden in piles of dusty junk. Finn blinked as his eyes slowly adjusted to the gloom. An old man stepped through a curtain hidden in the shadows. He peered suspiciously at them through thick reading glasses.

"Can I help you?" he muttered. "What brings you here?" The shopkeeper gasped when he saw the broken necklace Izzy held out to him.

He stepped backwards, away from them, his eyes glued on it fearfully.

"Well, he certainly doesn't look very happy to see us ... or that necklace," whispered Kit.

"It's beautiful," admitted the shopkeeper, "but it comes with the threat of terrible danger. Dark spies will be searching for it. They are servants of the old sorcerer, seeking what was lost."

Chapter 3: Danger in the Shadows

The shopkeeper stopped speaking suddenly, as if he regretted having spoken.

The word 'danger' triggered different responses in the three friends. Kit's eyes lit up and he looked at the necklace with renewed interest. Izzy gazed at it in horror. Finn wanted to find out more.

"Please, will you take a closer look at it, sir?" he begged. He stepped forward towards the retreating shopkeeper. At that moment a hooded figure leaped down from the rafters above them. He crashed into Finn and tried to snatch the necklace from Izzy's shaking fingers.

Kit rushed to help. He pushed hard against a tall bookcase. The heavy books rained down on the dark figure.

"Run!" hissed the shopkeeper. He pressed a scrap of paper into Finn's hand. "Follow the directions to the old town. The answers you seek are in the ruins of the old museum."

He gestured at the hooded figure, slumped
on the floor. "Make haste before this dark spy
wakes up," he urged. "Please, never return here.
This is the last time I will help you. I have
carried the weight of a terrible secret for many
years. It is your turn now to take it on."

With no time for discussion, they ran from the shop and raced along the streets. Monk clung silently to Finn's shoulder. Izzy knew this part of town well. She led them down a maze of dark alleyways. The other two soon had no idea where they were heading. The three of them looked nervously behind them as they ran. They were terrified of seeing the hooded figure following them.

"He's coming!" gasped Izzy suddenly, in panic. "There, beside those crates. He's looking for us!" They pressed themselves into a darkened doorway, hearts beating crazily.

"It's getting late," panted Kit. "The streets are emptying and he'll be able to see us!" He squinted upwards. "We'll have a better chance if we go across the rooftops!"

Izzy's face revealed her fear even before she spoke. "The rooftops, Kit? Are you joking? Monk might make it, but the rest of us will break our necks!"

Kit knew Izzy was terrified of heights. "Please, Iz," he said gently. "That dark spy isn't someone we want to meet in a hurry and he's about to spot us." He felt along the wall behind him. "This door is open. It's our escape route."

They slid through the door and raced up a flight of steps. Their feet clattered against the stone as they headed for the tiled roof.

"We'll need to jump from one rooftop to another," said Kit. "Treat it as a game," he urged Izzy. "Don't overthink it. Just take it one step at a time."

They raced along the rooftops, jumping from one building to the next. Izzy was white-faced with fear, but she kept up with the others. Years of traveling with her dad had taught her to be fast and nimble, especially in the face of danger.

It was easy at first as the buildings were close together. Suddenly they reached a place where they needed to jump across a huge gap to reach the next building. Izzy's face screwed up in fear.

"You can do it, Iz," urged Kit. "Just don't look down." The three of them leaped bravely towards the next building, but the gap was too wide.

Suddenly they were falling! A chill wind howled past their ears as they dropped rapidly towards the ground. There was no escape!

Finn reached desperately for Izzy's hand. Seconds away from crashing to the ground, their fall was softened by a huge canvas. It was stretched between the two buildings.

Chapter 4: An Amazing Discovery

They lay trembling in the safe hammock of canvas, winded and terrified by their fall. "That was close," gasped Finn.

"You can say that again," said Izzy. "It's too far to jump. Let's find a safe way down."

They peered down into the gloomy space below them.

Kit took the rope from around his waist. He threaded it through a metal hook in the wall beside them. One by one they used the rope to slowly lower themselves down. Finn peered around.

"It looks like we're in the ruins of an old courtyard," he whispered. He gazed up at a dark, ruined building.

"Luckily, we've lost that creepy spy!" added Izzy with relief. Finn nodded, but he couldn't shake off the feeling that something was watching them. The silent building around them felt full of dark secrets. It towered over them, as if waiting for them to make a move. "Let's move on," he urged the others.

"Finn!" gasped Izzy suddenly, pointing at the necklace in Finn's hand. "Look at the amber jewel!"

The jewel had begun to glow with a soft orange light. It started to vibrate. Odd shadows whirled inside it like a miniature tide.

"It's as if it is trying to help us," said Izzy in wonder. Finn held up the necklace.

The space around them slowly began to take shape in the strange orange light.

Kit had a sudden realization. "This is the courtyard of the ruined museum! We've landed exactly where we need to be!"

Kit led them across the courtyard and into the museum. The building had been in ruins for years. They explored a long corridor of locked wooden doors. Each one was guarded by a broken stone statue. Eventually they arrived at a heavy wooden door that opened into a huge hall.

Pools of colored light spilled onto the floor from a cracked stained-glass window. Izzy clutched Finn's arm and pointed across the hall. A huge golden map stretched across the dusty wall.

"It's a map of the ancient kingdom," whispered Izzy in amazement. "My father has talked about that place for years. I thought it only existed in his dreams. This must be what we've been sent to find!"

As they gazed at the map, the light from the amber jewel in Finn's hand began to vibrate more brightly. It seemed to be urging them even further onwards. The flickering orange light revealed a huge statue of a warrior holding a mighty sword.

Suddenly, Finn noticed a round purple orb in the warrior's hand. The orb was the size of a large orange. It was made of a totally different material to the rest of the statue. He saw a pulsing light deep inside it.

Chapter 5: A Strange Object

"We need to get that purple orb," Finn shouted. "There is some connection between it and the amber jewel in the necklace."

Kit wasted no time. He began to clamber up the stone statue, as nimbly as a spider. This was territory he knew well.

Kit clambered along the statue's arm like a panther on a thick tree branch. He began to inch towards the purple orb. It shimmered as he touched it. He tried to prise it loose using his climbing hook. It was no good. The orb was stuck fast in the statue's hand.

Suddenly a blinding light filled the hall. The massive door at the entrance was flung open. A horrifying cyclops appeared in the lit doorway. It glared crazily from one bloodshot eye in the middle of its forehead. It scanned the room.

At its side was the hooded spy! He was controlling the cyclops with a device. It gave out strange blue energy waves.

Under the control of the hooded spy, the cyclops lunged across the room. It began to attack the statue with a massive stone hammer.

The statue began to fracture. Huge shards of heavy gray rock rained to the ground. A sudden terrifying cracking sound filled the air.

The statue's stone arm crumbled and collapsed.
Kit was thrown off the statue in an explosion of
rubble.

"Kit!" yelled Izzy, in panic. The purple orb
tumbled to the ground. Izzy raced to grab it.

Izzy retreated into the shadows as a cloud of dust filled the room.

Finn handed Monk the necklace. "Take it to Izzy," he whispered. "This beast mustn't get the amber jewel, even if it gets me." He weaved crazily across the floor, trying to distract the cyclops away from the others. "Come on, monster. Follow me!" he yelled.

The cyclops struggled to track Finn with its one bleary eye. It swung its hammer wildly, trying to catch Finn.

Kit, winded from his fall, was lying in the dust. He stirred now and staggered to his feet. He threw himself bravely at the hooded spy, knocking him to the floor. The strange controlling device was lost in a sea of rubble.

Without the spy as his controller, the cyclops was filled with confusion. It shook its massive head from side to side. Thick strings of saliva sprayed from its disgusting mouth.

Monk ran to Izzy. He thrust the necklace into her hand. Instinct made her put it around her neck. She had a sudden strong feeling that the purple orb was calling to her. What was she supposed to do?

She ran her fingers over it. It made no sense to her. She noticed something strange. The orb was not complete. It had a deep empty socket at its center.

The amber jewel and the purple orb in her hand were both now pulsing wildly. Izzy grasped the amber jewel. She twisted it sharply and yanked it off the necklace. She thrust it into the empty socket in the purple orb.

Chapter 6: A Giant Creature

White mist poured from the purple orb. A giant winged creature slowly took shape before them. He flexed his muscular limbs and unfurled huge, powerful wings. The hooded spy retreated in terror and tripped over his feet as he raced for the doorway. The amber jewel dropped back out of the purple orb. Izzy jammed it back into the necklace.

The powerful winged creature had been released from the amber jewel! He reared up defiantly on his massive hind legs.

The puzzled cyclops backed away. It howled one last roar of confusion, then stumbled from the room. Finn felt the hairs on the back of his neck prickle with fear. Was this creature a friend or an enemy? He stepped forward bravely to face him.

The creature's flecked eyes softened. He spoke in a deep rumbling tone.

"The three of you have released me. I need to ask for your help, but I know it will place you in great danger."

Kit grinned. "We're in! Tell us what to do!"

"Should we?" Finn asked Izzy softly.

Joy and relief surged through Izzy. By some miracle they had escaped both a cyclops and a dark spy. Now they were being offered an adventure.

"You and Kit are my best friends. If you're in, then I'm in," she said with a grin.

The creature lowered his head towards them. "I am humbled by your trust. An evil sorcerer from the past has resurfaced. Our world is no longer safe. I am one of ten powerful Guardians," he told them. "You released me when you put the amber jewel into the orb in your hand. My nine friends are still trapped in amber jewels scattered across the ancient kingdom. Together, the ten of us can destroy the sorcerer and his dark forces."

He paused, his voice softening. "Will you come with me to the ancient kingdom and release the other Guardians?"

He stretched out his massive wings. "There is no time to lose. Take your places on my back and we can begin our quest … "

Glossary

affectionately	– lovingly, tenderly
amber	– a yellow or brown fossil resin often made into jewelry
bleary	– blurred or dimmed
browsing	– casually looking through things for sale
clamber	– climb using hands and feet
clattered	– made a loud, rattling noise
dismissively	– in a manner indicating that something or someone is not worth anything
emerged	– moved away from something and became visible
flexed	– tightened
fracture	– break or split
glinting	– giving out tiny, quick flashes of light
haste	– hurry

inseparable – can't be parted

instinct – a natural impulse, not thought through

irate – very angry

nimble – quick and light in movement

pulsing – throbbing

resurfaced – came to the surface again

shimmered – shone with a faint light

shudder – tremble with fear or cold

socket – a hollow part of something, designed for something else to fit into

squinted – looked with his eyes partly closed

thrust – shoved

unfurled – opened out from a folded state

urged – persuaded

The Bones of Ruin

Book 2

This book offers the reader the opportunity to read words with the suffixes ful, less, ness, er, est, ly, en, ish, y, able and ible.

Contents

Chapter 1: The Ten Guardians

They rode safely across the moonlit sky on the back of the winged Guardian. It was a ride none of the three friends would ever forget.

The creature introduced himself. "I am a Griffin. That purple orb in your pocket, Izzy, contains powerful magic. Rest now and I will tell you more of this quest while we travel.

"The ancient kingdom was once kept safe by ten Guardians. Each had their own immense power. An evil sorcerer yearned to control them. He created the orb to steal their spirits. The magic orb is very important. It can be used either to capture or to release the spirits. The sorcerer used the orb to imprison the spirits of the Guardians in ten amber jewels. He had them inserted into a marvelous necklace. Before he could harness their power, the dark forces of his experiments caused an awful explosion. It sent these amber jewels flying across the land.

"Only one of the jewels was left in the necklace. The destination of the orb and the necklace had always remained a mystery. Until now, no one knew what had happened to them.

"Friends of the Guardians spent many years searching for the amber jewels. When they found them, they built them into unusual monuments. They hoped this would hide them from the sorcerer and his dark spies.

"You have released me from the one jewel left in the necklace. You now need to find the nine monuments and collect each of the remaining amber jewels. When you insert the jewels into the orb, you will release the spirits of the Guardians. Keep the amber jewels in the necklace once their spirits have been released. That will keep them safe from the dark spies!"

The Griffin looked at them solemnly. "Be careful. The sorcerer has risen again and has many dark spies.

"The dark spies have found many of the monuments and are guarding them. They will stop at nothing to keep you away from them. They are still searching for the orb. If they find out you have it, you will be in terrible danger."

The Griffin flew on, through the dark hours of the night. His riders talked excitedly about his story before gradually falling asleep on his back. Finally, they landed on a rocky hillside, just as the sun was rising.

"Where are we?" Izzy asked groggily. She hugged herself against the chill of the early morning mist. The Griffin pointed around them with his golden claw.

"You will find an ancient map somewhere here. It will tell you where all the monuments to the old Guardians were built." His eyes glistened as he prepared to leave them. "I must prepare carefully for the battle that is to come," he said. He unfurled his great wings to take flight. "You have shown yourselves to be a fearless team. That will serve you well in the challenges you will have to face. Good luck, my friends."

Izzy noticed a beam of light seeping from the orb. A flickering image spilled onto the rocks next to them.

"It must be a clue to where the map is," said Kit hopefully. "It looks like a circle of shards and some sort of horn."

Finn was more apprehensive. "Those shards look more like teeth to me," he shuddered. "That horn image might well be a hunted animal."

Monk gulped and gripped Izzy's hand.

Chapter 2: Where is the Map?

They set off in search of the map, following a snaking pathway down the rocky hillside. "Some of these rocks look almost man-made," said Izzy thoughtfully.

"You're right, Iz!" said Kit. "These aren't rocks at all – they're ruins. I think we're in the remains of an ancient town!" They came across bigger and bigger ruins, looming out of the mist from both sides of the path.

Finn squinted up at the paint marks on the old buildings. "The map is likely to be in an important building. I wonder if these symbols can help us?" he said.

Monk had his own plan for finding the map. He scampered fearlessly into the mist, weaving his way nimbly through the ruins. He gestured eagerly for them to follow him. The sun rose higher and the mists began to clear. Monk led them down an alleyway and into a paved clearing.

"Welcome to the center of town!" grinned Kit. "Surely the map will be here." He pointed excitedly across the town square to a gloomy building opposite them. "I think that blackened ruin might be the town hall. Maybe it's in there?"

The jagged remains of the old town hall were just the sort of climbing challenge Kit enjoyed. He quickly began to scale a crumbling stone staircase in the heart of the building.

"Be careful!" called out Izzy.

At first Kit made good progress, but the old building had been weakened over time by the weather. A huge section of the crumbling staircase suddenly crashed to the ground. He was thrown off balance. He swung his climbing ax wildly. Luckily, he managed to find a hold in the ancient stone.

"I'm OK!" he called down. "But tread carefully. This staircase won't last much longer."

The three of them inched slowly up the remains of the staircase. At last they reached a balcony high up on the outside of the old town hall.

They paused to gaze down at the town, now far below them. The early morning light was spreading like melted butter over the parched cobbles of the town square. Finn shielded his eyes against the powerful glare of the rising sun.

"That spiral pattern of rocks round the fountain!" he said thoughtfully. "It's exactly the same shape as the spiral the orb showed us!"

"You're right, Finn!" said Kit eagerly. "The orb was giving us a clue! The map must be at that fountain! We need to get down there."

He gazed around him. Knotted vines hung from the building. Strands of ivy had crawled their way into the brickwork.

"These vines might be helpful. They're stronger than the stone," he said. "Climbing down these would be safer than using the stairs."

Izzy rolled her eyes. "Why do your ideas always involve climbing?" she asked. "No wonder Monk loves you!"

Finn did not join in with their laughter. He was troubled by a scrabbling noise he could hear coming from deep within the building. Were they being followed? Who would know they were here? His heart pounded painfully as he remembered the Griffin's awful warning about the dark spies.

A swinging vine was not a good place to meet another cyclops! The sooner they got back to the ground the better. "Let's go!" he urged.

He and Kit began to scramble carefully down the building. They swung more adventurously as they realized the tough ladders of vines could hold their weight.

Izzy paused and glanced fearfully behind her as she started to follow the others. Was that a shadowy figure watching them?

"I take it all back about climbing, Kit," Izzy

called out. "Let's go as fast as we can."

Safe on the ground again, they found themselves beside a row of old shops. Dusty boxes were piled untidily in the windows.

"The fountain's that way," urged Kit, pointing ahead of them. Izzy was distracted by a row of faded and musty books in one of the cracked windows. "Wait a second," she said. "This is an old bookshop. You often find maps in bookshops!"

It was worth a try. Kit leaned his shoulder against the door. A few hard pushes did the trick. The timber door creaked and gave way enough to create a narrow crack. Izzy squeezed carefully through the gap. Kit peered through the gap, searching for her among the shadows.

A sudden tapping made both boys jump. Izzy's grinning face appeared at a broken window.

"I've got it!" called Izzy, waving a folded wad of yellowed paper. "The map!"

Chapter 4: Things Take Shape

The ancient map rustled as she held it out to them. It opened stiffly, as if not quite ready to share its secrets.

It was the same map they had seen on the wall of the old museum. The map of the ancient kingdom! Careful ink drawings showed the position of all of the remaining Guardians.

"That dark shape there looks familiar," said Kit as he peered at the faded drawing. "It's the mountain near where my grandparents live. I've climbed there and I know the shape of that lake beside it."

Finn was tracing his finger slowly across the map from the shaded area Kit had identified. "If that's the mountain, then this could be the ruined town we're standing in," he said. He tapped his finger thoughtfully on the map as he started to piece it all together. His brain began to fizz in his head as things suddenly began to make sense to him.

"The ancient kingdom is closer to our world than I thought," he said excitedly. He looked up, his eyes glinting. "The ruins of the ancient kingdom were here all along. We just didn't know they existed."

Before the others could respond, two startling things happened. An awful screaming sound filled the air. At the same moment a tiny figure burst through a nearby shop window in a cloud of splintered glass and dust. A dark spy! He had been following them all along! Still screaming, he raced towards the fountain.

The three friends stared in shocked horror. The fountain was suddenly shrouded in an eerie blue light.

Finn gasped. "That spiral of rock shards around the fountain … It's moving!"

The shards of rock were indeed moving. Finn pointed in fear. The sea of fragments twisted and contorted. The rocks assembled into skeleton

warriors. White skulls glistened in the light as
the eyeless monsters stumbled towards them.

"We have to distract them!" yelled Finn. He
took a guess that these blind warriors would have
great sensitivity to sound and smell. Grabbing
two handfuls of pebbles, he darted forward.

"Here, my boney friends! Over here!" he bellowed. He scattered the rattling pebbles wildly so the noise would confuse them. The tribe of skeleton warriors froze for a second. They were confused by Finn's booming voice as it echoed off the buildings around them. They turned, raising their axes. They had caught Kit's scent now and were heading towards him.

Adrenalin powered through Kit as the creatures surged towards him. Ducking swiftly this way and that, he used his climbing ax to fight off their swords. Monk scooted crazily around, low to the ground. He launched himself at the warriors' legs. He knocked several warriors over, but it was hopeless. More skeletons quickly replaced them.

Overwhelmed by numbers, Monk and the boys were forced to retreat. They took cover in the old bookshop. "Where's Izzy?" gasped Finn, as they crouched fearfully in the doorway.

Chapter 5: Izzy Has a Plan

Izzy had plans of her own. She could see a small hooded figure by the fountain. A dark spy! He was controlling the skeleton warriors with a device held in his hand. It shot a pulsing energy across the courtyard.

"There must be some reason why the dark spy is over there," muttered Izzy. Hiding in patches of shadow, she crept towards the fountain.

Izzy scrambled onto the low walls of the magical fountain. The swirling water was deeper than it looked. In the center of the fountain were the remains of a broken statue.

"Stay away from there, human girl!" bellowed the dark spy. His snarling fury was much greater than his size. He leaped onto the broken statue and turned his device towards Izzy.

A surge of strange energy from his device hit Izzy like a hammer. It caught her on the shoulder. It was so painful that she almost fell over.

Izzy knew she had to get away. Gathering
her courage, she took a deep breath and
dived below the surface of the water. She
was desperately hoping the dark spy's strange
powers didn't work underwater.

Back at the bookshop, Monk and the boys were now in desperate trouble. They had wedged themselves inside a tiny space behind some wooden boxes. It was no good. The skeleton warriors were destroying their wall of boxes as easily as sweeping away cut grass.

"Run, Kit, and I'll distract them," hissed Finn. In that second, all movement around them suddenly stopped. The horde of warriors was now frozen. They were unable to move without the controlling force of the dark spy.

At the fountain, the dark spy's attack on Izzy was getting stronger. Flashes of energy fizzed around her. They nearly hit her! She plunged deeper underwater. A faint golden glow caught her eye. What could be glowing down here? Swimming deeper, she found the stone head from the broken statue. It was a beautiful Unicorn, crowned with a spiral horn. In the center of the horn was an amber jewel!

Surely this was the image the orb had been showing them!

Izzy tried to tug the jewel loose. It pulsed gently against her fingers, almost like a heartbeat. It would not budge. She needed air so badly that she nearly blacked out. She swam back upwards, quickly gasping huge gulps of air into her aching lungs as she surfaced.

Chapter 6: Bolts of Energy

The dark spy saw her surface. "No human will outwit me!" he snarled. He used his device to shoot out more harmful energy. Sparks fizzed and hummed in the water like electric eels.

Izzy gasped as she saw one of the bolts of energy strike the amber jewel. The force of the impact dislodged the jewel from the rock. It spiraled through the water. She dived down again and grasped the jewel. She clutched it to her chest as she swam to the surface. The orb shuddered in her pocket. Izzy grabbed it and slammed the amber jewel into the newly formed socket in its side.

A charge of energy, as fast as a bolt of lightning, shot out of the orb. It bathed the waters of the fountain in dazzling white light.

Finn and Kit leaped out of their hiding place in the old bookshop. They knocked away the dry bones of the static warriors that surrounded them.

The boys ran towards the fountain, shielding their eyes from the sudden blinding light.

"Is it a horse, Finn?" asked Kit as the fountain stirred in rainbows of light. A horned creature, with a flowing mane, rose from the waves.

As the dazzling light around the fountain cleared, the creature stepped proudly forward. "It's a Unicorn," whispered Finn in awe. "This adventure gets better and better!"

The Unicorn tossed his mane powerfully. He sent splashes of water over them all. He flicked the controlling device from the spy's hand with the tip of his horn. It fell into the swirling waters of the fountain.

"No!" bellowed the dark spy in disbelief. He was powerless now without his controlling device and his army of warriors. The magical waters of the fountain surged up, forming a powerful whirlpool. It dragged the dark spy deep into the swirling water.

The Unicorn barely glanced at the three friends huddled in awe before him. With a scornful snort, he shook his mane and galloped off. The last of the blazing light vanished as he passed through it.

The three of them slowly came out of their shocked trance. "Well, he was certainly different to the first Guardian!" laughed Kit. "It looks like you saved the day again, Izzy!"

Izzy tucked the second amber jewel into the necklace and hugged Kit warmly. "It was nothing. You know how much I like swimming. Today I was lucky enough to swim with a magical Unicorn!"

"Izzy, your shoulder!" gasped Finn as he looked at her.

"It's only a scratch," said Izzy. "I have some herbs in my pouch that will heal it." She opened the pouch of herbs thoughtfully. "This is a good place to store the necklace," she told them. "The Griffin told us to keep the jewels well hidden."

Monk darted around. He was throwing pebbles to topple the last remains of the skeletons.

Finn watched the Unicorn disappear into the mist. "Well, we survived our first challenge," he said. "Let's look at the map. I wonder where this crazy adventure is going to take us next."

Glossary

apprehensive   – uneasy and fearful about something that might happen

bellowed   – shouted in a loud, deep voice

contorted   – twisted in a violent way

distracted   – not concentrating, or paying attention to something else

dread   – great fear or reluctance

gestured   – signaled with his hand

glistened   – sparkled with light

groggily   – dazed and weak from lack of sleep

gulped   – swallowed fearfully

immense   – enormous, huge

impact   – collision

marvelous   – excellent or great

musty	– having a stale smell as in a room which has been closed for a long time with no fresh air
outwit	– cleverly get the better of someone
overwhelmed	– overpowered by something
parched	– hot and dry
piercing	– loud and shrill
plunged	– dived down
scampered	– ran about playfully
scrabbling	– scratching
static	– not moving
trance	– dazed or hypnotized state
unfurled	– opened out from a folded state
yearned	– had a strong desire

Into the Unknown

The City of
Epicantor

STRATOS MOUNTAINS

TITAN STRAITS

FALUCA JUNGLE

ARON STEPPES

The City of
Athelos

EMERA

BITTERBOON
MOUNTAINS

WASTELAND WILDERNESS

Book 3

This book offers the reader the opportunity to read words with the prefixes un, in, im, ir, il, dis and mis.

Contents

Chapter 1: An Icy Climb

The three friends sat on the low wall of the fountain. Finn unfolded the map to find the location of the next monument. "It's lucky you're here, Kit," he joked, as they set off. "The next jewel is up a mountain. We'll need your climbing skills to get us up it!"

An icy wind began to blow as they reached the base of a snow-capped mountain. They climbed steadily upwards, huddling together for warmth in the bitter cold. Monk tucked himself snugly inside Finn's cloak. He pulled the cloth tightly round his shivering body.

"Good idea, little guy," said Izzy, rubbing his head affectionately. "Looks like snow is coming."

They climbed for hours. Snow started gently, then began to fall more heavily. It made the way ahead almost invisible. Finn looked around. The setting sun cast long shadows across the snow. The sky was already growing dark.

"We need to find a place to camp for the night," he told Kit. "There's a cave on the other side of that bridge. Let's head for that."

The old wooden bridge had seen better days. Cracked and broken planks made it almost impossible to find a safe route across.

Luckily, Monk had a natural eye for a safe climbing route.

"Yet again our lives are in the hands of a little monkey," joked Kit. They followed Monk, clambering from one rotted plank to the next across the ruined bridge.

Suddenly a colony of bats burst out from the shadows under the bridge. A mass of tiny screeching bodies flew at their faces. It was hard to think clearly in the chaos.

Finn was struggling to see through the flurry of frantically beating wings. He almost fell into the deep gorge below the bridge. Izzy's quick reflexes saved him. She held Kit's hand for

support and reached out to grab Finn.

"Stick together!" Kit yelled. "We're nearly there."

Beating away the last of the bats, they clambered up the bank at the end of the bridge.

Chapter 2: A Hidden Mine

Finn could see a cave just ahead of them. He motioned to the others to head for it. Suddenly a terrifying rumbling filled the air. They whirled round in horror to see the bridge collapsing behind them. It dragged gravel and rocks deep down into the gorge below it.

A white tidal wave of snow was triggered by the vibrations of the collapsing bridge. It slid down the mountain towards them.

"Run, or we'll end up in that gorge!" yelled Finn urgently.

The three of them raced across the trembling mountainside to the safety of the cave.

It was dark inside the cave and almost impossible to see. Kit took a small tinder box from his bag and scratched at it to create a flame. Finn searched the cave floor for a thick stick. He held it over the flame to create a torch. Now they could inspect the cave.

The light from the torch threw everything into shadow. "I think I know where we are!" said Izzy nervously. "This is the Kontag gold mine! My father told me it was abandoned years ago. Rumor has it that a creature, known as a viperator, emerged from the depths of the gorge to take possession of it." She looked around her unhappily. "The orb is glowing," she said. Her voice trembled as she pulled it from her pocket. "I think our next monument is nearby."

Kit was already exploring the cave. He could see a tunnel leading right down into the mine.

"Come on! The next monument must be down here," he called impatiently. Monk chattered on his shoulder, pointing down into the shadows.

"Let's go!" yelled Kit. He crouched down and clambered into the narrow entrance. They scrambled through a series of narrow tunnels. Finally they arrived at a rocky ledge supported by thick timber posts. The light from the torch showed glimpses of something far below them in the shadows.

"I can't make out what that is," said Kit as he peered into the gloom, "but there's a faint amber glow down there. That must be a good sign!"

"A good sign? Or a sign we might be about to meet that viperator?" muttered Izzy uncertainly.

Her foot knocked a rock into the inky darkness below the ledge. A splash echoed around them as the rock hit water far below. "My father told me the mine flooded a while back," she added unhappily. "It sounds like the water is still there."

Finn glanced behind him. He shuddered as he caught a glimpse of something scaly and muscular rippling in the shadows. A strange rumbling filled the air. Clouds of dust fell unexpectedly from the ceiling. Something unknown was sliding rapidly through the tunnels around them.

"We need to move on from here," he urged the others. "We're not safe here."

Chapter 3: A Terrifying Encounter

Monk took the lead. The others instinctively followed behind him. They ran along a framework of rickety wooden bridges. They were heading deeper into the mine. Symbols had been etched into some of the wooden frames they passed under. Kit paused at one. He traced the symbols gently with his fingers.

"These markings all mean something," he said. His voice was rising with excitement. "The individual paths are all connected. These symbols are a map of the mine." Kit had an amazing memory for directions. He picked up a stick. He began to scratch out their route in the dust on the bridge. "I am sure we are near the bottom," he told Izzy. "The amber jewel will be close by."

The rumbling sounds suddenly intensified. An eerie hiss echoed unpleasantly through the gloom. Something or someone was very close to them.

"Put the torch out now," whispered Izzy. "We stand a better chance if we are invisible." They put the torch out and began to run faster. They felt their way along the walls as they raced towards the water at the bottom of the mine.

The unnerving hissing noise increased. It was accompanied by a strange dragging sound. Finn felt more and more uncomfortable. Whatever was chasing them was gaining ground.

"We're nearly at the bottom of the mine shaft!" gasped Finn at last. "I can smell the water."

They paused briefly for breath in a small chamber. They had been in the tunnels all night. Shafts of morning light came from above them, illuminating the mine. The air around them smelled foul. The walls here were wet with a tacky slime.

The eerie dragging sound in the tunnels continued to confuse Finn. It sounded like water rushing uphill, but that was impossible. How could water be running uphill?

It was not liquid rushing towards them. It was something living and breathing and filled with cold, venomous fury.

The three friends shrieked in fear as a huge scaly serpent suddenly appeared out of nowhere! It lunged at them. Its huge jaws opened to reveal a forked red tongue that flicked aggressively towards them.

"It's the viperator!" yelled Izzy in terror. They

staggered back, away from its massive jaws.

The edge of Finn's tunic was caught in its vast razor-like teeth! "Get off him!" yelled Izzy. She yanked Finn away from the snapping jaws. They turned and fled.

Izzy looked quickly behind them as they ran. The huge creature was horrifyingly close behind them. Coil after coil of its glistening body slid out of the mist. It rippled powerfully towards them.

Chapter 4: Into the Unknown

They turned a sharp corner and ran on again. Kit led them on a crazy path through the mine. His understanding of the layout of the mine helped them stay just one step ahead of the serpent.

The bridge beneath their feet trembled with the weight of the enormous beast as it slithered after them.

"Quick, in here!" yelled Kit as they stumbled past a shadowy cave in the wall. "If we stay quiet, it might go straight past us. Snakes have poor memories. It might forget we're the enemy."

They knew it was a slim chance, but the three of them ducked into the small dark space. Kit dragged a huge rock into the opening as a barricade.

They stood immobile, as still and silent as statues. A loud crashing sound soon told them that the viperator had not forgotten them. It was attacking their barricade.

Finn looked around wildly. He discovered there was no wall in the shadowy space behind them. They were standing on a ledge in front of a misty void. There was no way of knowing what lay in the darkness.

Finn gazed fearfully as he watched Kit and Monk exchange glances. Kit grabbed Monk's hand and they leaped impulsively off the thin ledge, straight into the unknown.

The huge rock they had put up as a barricade began to tremble. The viperator's terrifying hissing filled the space around them. It sounded like a swarm of angry bees.

"We have to follow Kit!" screamed Izzy.

The sight of a monstrous red tongue flicking around the edge of the rock convinced Finn she was right. He grasped Izzy's hand and together the two of them leaped into the void.

The viperator crashed through the barricade. It hissed in fury as it heard Finn and Izzy land loudly in the stagnant water below.

The icy water slammed into Finn. It felt like an attack by a thousand knives. Finn was overwhelmed with panic. Even though he was a fisherman, being underwater in the dark was something that terrified him.

Weeds grasped at his ankles, pulling him further underwater. His muscles froze. He couldn't pull himself back up to the surface.

In the last seconds of his consciousness, he felt slender arms slip under his armpits. They held him securely and pulled his head above water. Izzy had swum down to him. She was steadily pulling him up, out of the stagnant water.

They clambered out of the water onto a sandy shore. "Never set out on an underwater adventure without me, Finn," gasped Izzy. Finn hugged her gratefully. She had just saved his life.

Chapter 5: An Exotic Temple

Kit and Monk had survived their leap into the unknown. They swam quickly through the foul-smelling water. Cracks in the rocks let in splinters of light. The three friends gazed around them as their eyes adjusted to the gloom.

The remains of an ancient temple towered above them. It had been hidden deep underground for centuries.

Within seconds, Monk was clambering up a flight of enormous stone steps. The steps were decorated with the same symbols they had seen earlier. They raced to follow him. "Monk's found the way again!" grinned Kit.

The three friends raced breathlessly up the stone stairway. They found themselves inside an impressive rotunda with a high domed ceiling.

The orb made a sudden sharp movement inside Izzy's pocket. She drew it out into the gloomy light. A new image shone inside it.

"It's the same shape as this domed building," she said slowly. "I think I understand it. The amber jewel must be somewhere in here!"

Sadly, the rotunda around them was totally empty. "Maybe the special thing about this monument is that it's invisible," joked Kit. They kicked at the dusty floor, searching for clues.

Monk suddenly startled them by chattering excitedly from high above them in the roof.

"Monk, you clever thing! You knew exactly what the orb was showing!" beamed Izzy. She pointed up into the domed roof. There was an incredible painted mural across the whole ceiling.

An impressive bird with vast golden wings was painted in the center of the mural. It was surrounded by a mass of hissing snakes.

Izzy pointed excitedly at the enormous bird. "Look at the tattoo on the bird's chest!" she gasped. "It's painted with snake venom. Snake charmers paint them on themselves to protect them from the snakes they are taming. That bird is Ignia, the legendary snake charmer!"

Kit squinted up at the tattoo on Ignia's chest.

"That's interesting! We've seen that design
before," he said. "It's the same symbol we have
seen everywhere in the mine." Kit was a
puzzle-solver. His voice was rising with excitement.
He made an intelligent guess. "It has to be a
clue! Can you see the biggest snake in the
painting? It has that design all along its back!"

Finn almost exploded with excitement as his
eyes followed Kit's finger. "That snake's eye ... it's
the amber jewel!" he yelled.

Chapter 6: Frozen in Fear

Kit wasted no time. He untied his climbing rope and threw the grapple upwards. It caught securely in a crack in the ceiling.

Within seconds, he was clambering up the rope like a spider. The next amber jewel was almost within reach.

A terrifying hissing sound suddenly echoed round the room. Kit froze in terror on his climbing rope. He knew only one creature down here made that sound. He hung from the ceiling, swaying slowly back and forth. The only sound in the room was the creak of his rope.

A scrabbling sound above them drew all their eyes upwards. A giant crack appeared in the mural above Kit's head.

With a thundering crash, the ceiling split open. Dust and rocks poured into the room. Kit kept his eyes on the amber jewel. By some miracle, the splitting ceiling had dislodged it. He swung his

rope furiously towards it, flying through the air.
He was trying to catch the amber jewel as it fell.

At that moment, the serpent's mighty head burst
through the crack in the ceiling. Its huge jaws
were wide open. Finn and Izzy could only watch
in horror as the mighty serpent dropped from
the ceiling. It coiled like a hideous living scarf
around Kit's hanging body. Kit was being crushed
like dry twigs inside the coils of the viperator.

"Bite it, Finn," yelled Kit. "Find the tip of its tail and bite it!"

Finn leaped up onto the end of the snake's twisting body. He crawled his way to the end of its tail. He seized the tip of the tail in both hands. He bit down on it with all the strength in his jaw. The end of the snake's tail cracked sharply under the impact of his bite.

The viperator hissed in pain. It released its grip on Kit. It fell heavily to the floor, taking Finn with him.

Kit swung across the room on his rope. He leaped off it and raced to safety in the shadows.

Izzy had seen the amber jewel drop to the floor. It was lost in a swirling confusion of dust and rubble. The mine was collapsing. "I have to find the jewel and free the Guardian trapped inside it," she said grimly. "It's our only chance of escape."

Monk disappeared into the darkness. Seconds later, he emerged. He was holding the amber jewel!

The huge viperator recovered fast from the pain in its tail. It thrashed around the rotunda with renewed energy. It was now intent on catching the two boys cowering in the shadows. If ever they needed a Guardian, it was now!

Izzy jammed the jewel quickly into the orb. She stepped back in amazement as a stream of pure white light poured from inside it. The temple was filled with a spiraling coil of white mist.

Chapter 7: Ignia Takes Flight

The swirling mist cleared to reveal Ignia flying above them. The majestic bird cocked her head on one side. She was listening to the hiss of the recovering serpent. Unfurling her enormous golden wings, she zoomed down towards the thrashing viperator.

Ignia stared deeply into its eyes and the serpent fell into a sudden deep trance. The great bird snatched up its limp body with her hooked claws and soared upwards. She flew out of the temple and up over the inky underground water.

"That slippery beast stands no chance against Ignia, the snake charmer!" whooped Kit. They watched Ignia drop the serpent into the icy water. Finn and Izzy hugged in relief, unable to believe the snake had really gone. Finn handed Izzy the jewel that had just dropped from the orb.

Ignia turned gracefully in the air. She landed back gently beside them.

"I have a feeling she might be offering us a lift," whispered Kit. Ignia stretched out her wings before them, like an amazing fiery carpet.

They clambered onto the bird's broad back. A terrifying hissing sound suddenly echoed across the cavern. The icy water had broken the trance! The viperator was swimming back to the shore, its huge jaws open.

Ignia drew her wings in close, shielding the important riders crouched on her back. She flew upwards, bursting through the remains of the temple. She soared out of the mine.

Looking down, Finn caught a last glimpse of the viperator. It was twisting in thrashing fury beside the water. Its body was trapped in rocky debris as the mine collapsed.

Ignia flew on, out of the collapsing mine and over the mountain. Monk snuggled back into Finn's coat. He was asleep in seconds.

"You saved my life back there, Finn," said Kit gratefully.

Finn grinned. "Who knew a snakebite could also mean a human biting a snake!"

Glossary

barricade	– barrier constructed quickly to stop an enemy
clambering	– climbing using hands and feet
coils	– connected rings or spirals
consciousness	– the state of being conscious
fled	– ran away from danger
flurry	– sudden confusion
fury	– violent anger or rage
gloom	– (of light) total or partial darkness
grapple	– a hook for seizing hold of something
hideous	– very ugly, revolting
huddling	– gathering close together
illuminating	– lighting up
impact	– forceful collision of two things
impressive	– arousing awe and respect
impulsively	– without thinking about it first

instinctively – acting on impulse, not learned or thought through

lunged – moved forward quickly and suddenly

reflexes – involuntary, automatic reactions to a stimulus

rotunda – round building or room, usually with a dome

scrabbling – scratching

securely – safely

slithered – slid along a surface

stagnant – stale and foul (water) caused by it not flowing or running

unfurling – opening out from a folded state

vast – huge, enormous

venom – poison that snakes can introduce into people by biting

void – empty space

Roots of Corruption

Book 4

This book offers the reader the opportunity to read words with prefixes that relate to time, such as 're' and 'pre'.

Contents

Chapter 1: Pulled from the Sky

Flying through the night sky was both exciting and terrifying. The three friends had to shout to hear each other above the racing noise of the wind.

"Grab some sleep while you can!" yelled Finn. Izzy was too excited to sleep. She was remembering all the adventures they had been through.

They arrived at their next stopping point at sunrise. Finn peered down. "There is forest everywhere," he called out, "but that patch there looks exactly the same shape as the one on the map."

Kit was keen to get back to the quest. He bent forward to reach Ignia's ear. "Can you find a place for us to land?" he asked.

Ignia scanned the forest for a safe landing place. She hovered above a patch of tall trees, looking for a clearing in the forest.

"Her wings are so huge. If she needs to, she can stay aloft for hours, without beating them once," said Kit in awe.

"Is climbing not enough for you any more, Kit?" teased Izzy. "Are you trying to work out how to fly now?"

Their joking came to an abrupt stop as Ignia suddenly gave a massive shudder. The mighty bird began to plummet downwards!

Finn scanned the forest below them. There was no wind, but the trees below them were swaying violently. "These trees are like wild animals!" he yelled in terror. Spiked branches clutched at Ignia as if they were trying to drag her from the sky!

Ignia could not pull herself free from the branches. She smashed through the trees and crashed to the ground below.

Powerless to stop herself, the mighty bird careered across the forest floor. The trees clawed at her with branches as strong as muscular arms.

Vines whipped out of the foliage like long ropes. They wound themselves round Ignia. Only her size and the speed of her fall saved her from being captured. She crashed through the wild undergrowth. Finally, she came to a halt in the clearing they had seen from the sky.

"Ignia is hurt!" sobbed Izzy as she scrambled down from her back. "She's unconscious!"

Chapter 2: Into the Forest

One of Ignia's wings was painfully distorted. It sat at an odd angle to the rest of her limp body.

Finn gently examined it. "It's not broken, but it's badly twisted," he said. "Something very strange is happening. It's losing its color!"

The fire colors of the damaged wing slowly faded. Within seconds, it was gray and lifeless.

"We have to find a way to restore her colors," sobbed Izzy. "There will be herbs in the forest strong enough to do it."

Finn eyed the swaying trees around them suspiciously. He had a premonition that 'healing' was not what this forest had in mind.

The orb began to judder. Izzy turned it around. "One of the symbols is glowing!" she said. "It looks like some sort of waterfall."

Finn looked around anxiously. Was the forest closer than before? Was it advancing towards them?

Kit was quick to respond. "We must find the amber jewel," he said. "But we can't leave Ignia unprotected." He built a small campfire as a precaution. "This will prevent any unwelcome visitors," he said.

They set off into the dense forest.

Tall pine trees blocked out the sunlight. It was slow and exhausting fighting their way through the dense undergrowth. They stopped to rest under a huge tree. Its branches stretched high above the rest of the forest.

"I'll climb it," said Kit. He began to clamber up the massive tree trunk. "I might see some landmarks to follow from up here."

Kit climbed so fast that he lost his footing and almost fell! He dangled from a branch. Monk reacted quickly. He scampered up the tree and thrust another, thicker branch towards Kit.

"Sometimes I wish Kit would be just a bit less brave," Izzy whispered to Finn.

Shaken by his fall, Kit paused and then resumed his climb. This time he went more carefully. Finally, he reached the top. "I can see the whole forest from here!" he yelled in amazement.

Kit gazed ahead of him. The early morning mist was clearing. At the edge of the forest was an enormous waterfall.

"I know which way to go!" Kit shouted down. "I can see the waterfall that was on the orb. There's a huge monument there too. We need to head that way."

Kit began to climb back down, describing a series of tall obelisks he had seen ahead of them in the forest. "The obelisks lead to the monument. We can follow them!" he called out excitedly. He stepped onto a broad branch.

The branch suddenly shot backwards! Kit jumped quickly to the safety of another branch. That branch thrust sharply forward, throwing him out of the tree!

Monk screamed in terror as he saw Kit drop downwards. The sharp branches of the tree seemed to be snatching at him as he fell. Kit just managed to grab hold of another branch. He hung underneath it like a monkey.

Finn ran to help Kit. He pressed his body against the lower branches of the tree. He was able to stop them moving just long enough for his friend to drop safely to the ground.

The three friends raced off in search of the first obelisk. "I hope you can remember the route, Kit," gasped Izzy anxiously.

Kit caught a glimpse of stone through the trees. "I knew it!" he whooped. The first obelisk! It was covered in carved symbols.

The symbols didn't interest Kit. He wanted

to get to the top of it. He and Monk clambered
nimbly up the obelisk. They were determined to
spot the next one along the route to the waterfall.

They followed the line of obelisks through the
forest. Kit and Monk scrambled up each one to
see the location of the next.

Kit was enjoying this challenge, but Monk
was still frightened. He glanced behind him as
they ran, aware of rustling leaves behind them.

Chapter 3: The Forest is Alive

Now and again, the sound of beating drums and strange music drifted across the forest. It made them all uneasy. After a while, it faded and then stopped.

"Don't worry, Iz," Finn reassured her. "I think whatever it is has moved on."

The next obelisk came into view across a clearing. "Race you, Finn!" yelled Kit with a grin. They were running to reach it when Finn suddenly stumbled and fell.

A sinister root had risen from the ground and curled itself tightly around Finn's foot. The roots were trying to trap Kit too. He bent down and tore them off his ankles. He grinned as he looked up again. "This forest really doesn't like us!" he said to Izzy.

Izzy looked around in sudden panic. "Finn's disappeared! I think those roots have taken him!"

Finn was nowhere to be seen. They looked

around frantically. Where was he?

"There he is!" screamed Izzy suddenly. Finn
was being dragged under a massive tree close to
the obelisk.

Kit looped his climbing rope into a lasso. He
sent it spinning through the air. The circle of
rope hooked tightly over Finn's feet, just as he
was about to disappear under the roots.

"Let me help!" shouted Izzy. They pulled hard on the rope. Between them, they managed to yank Finn back out from under the roots.

Finn stumbled up groggily, his heart beating wildly. There was more danger on the horizon. A mass of roots was now slithering towards them. Finn searched desperately for a means of escape.

"There are no roots on the obelisk!" he yelled. "Climb it, quick!" With Monk clinging onto his shoulder, Finn clambered up the obelisk. He reached behind him to help pull Izzy up. Kit was seconds behind them.

Panting with exhaustion, the three of them huddled together on the obelisk. Below them, the seething mass of roots had surged to the base, but no further.

"They can't climb it!" said Kit in relief.

Suddenly, the strange drumming they had heard earlier rang out across the clearing. It was louder now and more insistent.

It seemed their troubles were not yet over.

The three friends gazed down fearfully from the top of the obelisk. The whole forest seemed to be shuddering below them. A wave of destruction rippled through the trees.

Chapter 4: Monstrous Root Creature

Suddenly, a howling monster burst through from the mess of broken branches. It headed straight for the base of the obelisk. The creature stood as tall as the trees and seemed almost to be one of them. It had huge muscular limbs and burning red eyes.

The creature roared as it smashed a timber fist into the side of the obelisk. Shards of splintered stone flew in all directions and narrowly missed Izzy's leg.

"The obelisk is going to collapse!" screamed Izzy. The three of them frantically scrambled back down it. They leaped off as they reached the base. They were in luck. They landed on a carpet of soft moss, just out of sight of the bellowing tree monster.

"I can hear the waterfall," said Izzy as they staggered to their feet. "It's nearby." They ran madly in the direction she was pointing.

The bizarre tree creature blundered clumsily after them. It hurled rocks and stones at them as it ran.

Monk scooted along close to the ground. He found them a route through the undergrowth which kept them one step ahead of the creature.

They reached the edge of the forest and stepped out at the top of the enormous waterfall. A pathway of rocky ledges looped around the edge of it. Water poured over the ledges. On the far side was an enormous structure. It was the same shape as the obelisks.

"Is that the next monument?" gasped Finn.

Before anyone could answer, the trees around them were torn up by the roots. The tree monster burst out of the forest behind them.

Finn quickly swung Monk up onto his shoulder. The three friends began to leap across the rocky ledges at the top of the waterfall. They ducked in and out of the water as they jumped.

Izzy looked behind them. "It can't get across!" she cried out with relief. "Its feet can't cling to these rocks!" The tree creature was struggling. Izzy was right. Its root-like feet were slithering on the wet, slippery rock.

"It's struggling, but it is still coming," said Kit grimly, "and there's more trouble up ahead. Look! The dark spies!"

Finn looked ahead of them. Kit was right. Two dark spies were huddled together on a ledge below them. They were playing strange instruments.

"That's where that strange singing and drumming was coming from," guessed Finn. "I bet those spies are the ones controlling both the forest and that crazy tree demon." He pulled his friends quickly out of sight behind a curtain of gushing water. "Listen. I have a plan."

Chapter 5: A Dangerous Plan

Finn quickly whispered his plan. Izzy groaned when she heard they were going to split up.

"It's a great plan, Finn," she said. "But if something happens to one of us, we're on our own."

Finn hugged her tight. "I'm scared too, Iz, but we'll always be close enough to help each other. You and Kit just dragged me out of those roots with a lasso. I trust you two with my life!"

Finn crept out of hiding first, taking a new lower pathway. Izzy climbed up onto a ledge above the others. Kit and Monk continued on their original route.

The bellowing tree creature had its red eyes locked on Kit. Its root-like feet were struggling on the slippery wet stones.

Finn was underneath the tree monster now. He was ready and prepared for the next stage of his plan. He needed to distract the creature away from Kit.

"Come on, plant monster!" he yelled.

The monster roared down at him. It swung its huge wooden fist. It was trying to knock Finn off the ledge.

Izzy stopped when she was directly above the tree monster. She hurled handfuls of grit and stones down onto it. She used her feet to kick loose stones off the rocky ledge. A shower of stones rained down on the tree monster. The monster roared in outrage as it struggled to keep its footing.

Kit seized his chance while the tree monster was distracted. He needed to get to the spies.

"Let's do it," whispered Kit. Grinning at each other, he and Monk leaped down onto the spies. They knocked them off the ledge and straight into the waterfall!

The strange musical instruments rolled over the edge of the waterfall too. They were smashed to pieces in seconds.

The strange power the spies had held over the tree monster stopped when the instruments were destroyed.

The monster swiftly turned back into the

ancient tree it had once been. Its roots buried themselves into the stone at the edge of the waterfall.

Finn gazed at the tree. "I am glad we freed you from the power of those dark spies," he said softly.

Chapter 6: Healing Guardian

The friends reunited at the far side of the waterfall. They were standing in front of the imposing monument. The stone structure was sheltering a beautifully carved wooden figure. She was dressed in elegant robes and had long flowing hair. The amber jewel was easy to see. It was tucked neatly into her chest, exactly where a heart might be.

Finn scrambled up the carving. He eased the amber stone gently from its resting place. Izzy wedged it excitedly into the orb.

The orb shimmered gently, releasing tiny dots of light. The dots floated upwards and clung to the wooden carving. A beautiful creature emerged from the light as the carving gradually came to life.

The Guardian's voice rustled like fall leaves as she introduced herself. "I am Refolia," she murmured, "a spirit of the earth."

Refolia stepped gently away from the waterfall and headed towards the forest.

Izzy glanced down at Monk. The monkey seemed oddly at ease. His hand rested gently on Refolia's ankle as he scampered along beside her.

"I must see you on to the next part of your quest," said Refolia warmly. She stretched out her fingers. A sea of roots rose up from the forest floor. Refolia gently wove them into a swaying rope bridge.

Izzy tugged Finn's sleeve. "We need to find a cure for Ignia," she reminded him.

"Ignia," murmured Refolia softly. She knelt down and pushed her hands deep into the earth. A carpet of flowers sprang from the forest floor. It spread rapidly around them.

Refolia laughed at their confused expressions. "Flowers are rich with nectar," she explained.

She raised her hands from the soil and clapped them lightly. A swarm of bees rose from the wild flowers. It drifted gently towards the forest. "I have asked them to take some of their honey back to Ignia. It has great healing powers," she told them.

The friends hugged Refolia gratefully as they prepared to leave.

Finn looked around as he stepped onto the bridge. Where was Monk? A puzzled shrug from Kit confirmed that he wasn't with him.

Izzy pointed to a rock nearby. Monk was

sitting quietly, in the middle of a family of tiny monkeys just like him. "I think perhaps Monk has made a different decision," she said gently.

Finn's heart flipped in his chest. After all they had gone through, had Monk decided to leave them?

"Monk probably comes from a forest like this one," explained Refolia gently. "He is welcome to make his home here with us if he chooses to."

Finn was shaking with sadness at the thought of saying goodbye to his friend. He knew in his heart that he must let Monk go if he chose it. He bent down to face the little monkey.

"We'd never have had this adventure without you, little guy," he said. "These monkeys are offering you a home. I respect your decision. I'll understand if you want to stay."

Monk looked quietly up at Finn. He did not move away from the other monkeys.

Tears filled Finn's eyes, but he stepped bravely onto the bridge behind Izzy. He had taken two steps when Monk clambered up onto his shoulder, chattering excitedly.

"Looks like it's going to be the four of us for a while longer!" grinned Kit.

Glossary

abrupt   – sudden or unexpected

blundered – moved about unsteadily

dense   – something where the parts of it are packed or crowded closely together

glanced   – looked quickly

groggily   – feeling tired

halt   – a sudden stop

haste   – urgent speed, a rush

insistent   – demanding, never giving up

lasso   – rope with a loop at one end, used for catching animals

moss   – tiny plants growing close together like a carpet on the ground, trees or rocks

nectar   – sugary liquid in a plant, which attracts insects or birds

nimbly   – moving easily with quick, light movements

obelisk	– four-sided monument tapering at the top
plummet	– plunge down
premonition	– feeling of anticipation or anxiety about a future event
reassured	– offered confidence and support
restore	– bring something back to original state
resumed	– carried on or continued (after interruption)
reunited	– joined again after separation
rustling	– slight, soft sounds as when things are rubbing together
seething	– in a state of agitation or excitement
shuddering	– trembling
sinister	– threatening or harmful
timber	– wood from trees

Trials and Trickery

The City of
Epicantor

ST

TITAN STRAITS

FALUCA JUNGLE

ARON STEPPES

EMERALD FALLS

The City of
Athelos

WASTELAND WILDERNESS

BITTERBOON
MOUNTAINS

Book 5

This book offers the reader the opportunity to read words with prefixes that relate to number, such as 'uni', 'tri' and 'quad'.

Contents

Chapter 1: United Once More

The swaying rope bridge took the three friends away from the waterfall and back through the forest. Finally, they reached the clearing where they had left Ignia.

The beautiful firebird was healed! Her wing was strong and golden again. The sight of a cloud of bees in the air above her reminded them that it was their sticky honey that had saved her.

"The day is nearly over," warned Ignia, as they settled once again on her feathery back. "We need to reach the next monument before nightfall."

They soared out of the forest. "I hope we're heading somewhere a bit more welcoming if we're going to spend the night there," Izzy called to the others.

Finn and Kit were hunched over the map. The next monument was puzzling. "The Misty Steps," read Finn thoughtfully. "It's right on the edge of the ancient kingdom. It's hard to tell from this drawing if those wavy lines mean it's on land or sea."

A sudden wind roared around them, spitting gritty dust and making it hard to see. Kit shielded his eyes against the growing dust storm. He peered down.

"There's a circle of tall rocks in that clearing," he yelled. "We can camp there."

The howling wind made for a bumpy landing. Vertical fingers of stone reached up into the sky around them. They were taller than their heads in some places.

"You saved my life in that forest and that will not be forgotten," said Ignia gratefully. "I must leave you now to join the other Guardians. We will meet again at the final battle."

Night was falling and the storm of dust and grit still swirled around them. Crouching low, they felt their way through the towering rocky shapes. At last they reached a cluster of smaller stones where they could set up camp.

Kit grinned as they settled down to sleep. "It might be windy, but at least there's no sign of life here!" he said in relief.

Chapter 2: The Dust Storm

By morning, the dust storm had died down, but the air was heavy with the threat of rain. "A storm is coming," said Finn nervously. "I hope this next monument is easy to find."

The orb suddenly shuddered. An image of a flight of stairs shone onto the rocks in front of them. "The Misty Steps!" guessed Izzy. "It looks as if we're in the right place."

The land around them looked as if the earth had been churned over by an earthquake. It grew rockier as they walked on. All signs of grass gradually disappeared. Gray mist seeped out from between the rocks below their feet. It curled gently around their legs.

By noon, the sandstorm had started again. Gritty sand battered them from all sides. It was hard for them to hear each other. Izzy tucked the orb into her pouch of herbs to keep it safe.

Suddenly she heard a sobbing sound. It was coming from behind them. "It sounds like a lost child!" she yelled. "We must try and help." She turned back, trying to find the source of the sobbing.

Izzy's voice was lost in the wind. Finn and Kit didn't hear her. They had no idea she had turned back. The boys struggled on through the dust storm for a few more minutes. Monk suddenly scampered up to them, his eyes wide with fear. He pointed wildly back in the direction they had come from.

"Izzy's gone!" yelled Finn. "She might be hurt. We must turn back!"

They frantically retraced their steps. Kit squinted into the swirling dust. Monk began to chatter excitedly. He had heard Izzy's voice!

Monk scampered into a patch of trees. "Follow Monk!" yelled Kit.

They ran after Monk. "Listen," whispered Finn suddenly. The sound of mumbled conversation drifted towards them. They crept forward slowly and peered through the trees.

Izzy was sitting against a tall tree. She was being guarded by two dark spies. The crying sound had been a trick! She had been captured!

The smell from a pot of stew cooking on a low fire drifted across to them. Finn grabbed Kit's arm and pointed. One of the dark spies was holding the orb! Finn pointed again. Izzy's pouch of herbs was hanging from a branch. The necklace was in that pouch! They had to get it before the spies found it.

Monk was the first to take action. He edged

his way across the clearing. He clambered up into the tree, above Izzy. Silently, he unhooked Izzy's pouch of herbs and dropped it gently into her lap.

Izzy reached quietly into the leather pouch. She pulled out a small cloth bag and quickly leaned forward. She grinned as she poured a stream of small yellow seeds into the pot of stew. Mustard seeds were a powerful laxative if taken in excess. "Now we just need to wait," she whispered to Monk with a grin.

The spies tucked into the bowls of stew. They gulped down the hidden mustard seeds without noticing them. It did not take long for the laxative to work. Both spies groaned with pain as they stumbled into the woods. A horrible smell confirmed that the mustard seeds had worked!

Izzy took her chance and ran. She and Monk quickly rejoined the others.

"There will never be another escape plan like that one!" joked Finn as he hugged her.

"The dark spies still have the orb. We need to get to the next amber jewel before they do," said Kit. They set off once again. They knew the spies would be hot on their heels.

Back at their camp, the spies were swiftly recovering. Tucking the orb into his coat, the taller of the two spies sniggered unpleasantly.

"Time for the golem, I think," he told his friend.

The spies headed for the strange rocks where Izzy and the boys had camped the night. One of

them aimed a controlling device at the rocks.

The rocks shuddered and then began to move! They rose up out of the splitting earth and joined together. The two spies giggled wildly.

A massive stone monster rose up from the earth. His clumsy body of rocks was cemented together with mud. The circle of strange stones had really been the limbs of a giant stone golem!

Chapter 3: A Rocky Route

The first warning Kit and the others had of the stone creature was a rippling shudder in the ground beneath their feet.

Izzy stumbled and fell. "Is it an earthquake, Finn?" she gasped as she staggered to her feet.

Finn turned to answer her. His mouth dropped open in horror. In the distance was a massive stone beast! It was heading their way!

"It's a golem!" Finn yelled. "A stone creature with no heart! It's heading our way! RUN!"

The rocks beneath them shuddered as the golem drew closer, but they stayed in place. "These rocks are designed like this for a reason," panted Kit as they ran.

Izzy peered closely at the rocks. "Kit, the ones in front of us are different. There are symbols scratched into them!"

A sea of stepping stones with symbols on stretched before them. Gray mist swirled around

the stones. "Maybe we're getting nearer the Misty Steps?" said Finn.

Kit leaned forward to peer at the stones. 'The stones are in patterns of four," he said thoughtfully. He stepped forward onto one to investigate. The stone under his foot suddenly dropped into the misty abyss below, almost taking Kit with it! Finn just managed to grab him and pull him to safety. Izzy gasped as the stone dropped far into the mist below them, way out of sight. It left a huge hole where it had just been.

"There's nothing under these rocks!" yelled Izzy in terror. "Where is the land?" The mist around them was shifting and thickening. It really did seem as if the rocky path was now floating in the clouds!

Finn peered into the distance. He grabbed Izzy's arm in amazement. "Izzy – look straight ahead. It's the Misty Steps!"

An enormous stairway was indeed now visible in the mists in front of them. It burst from the sea of hexagonal stones around it and led way up into the sky. The top of the steps was hidden in heavy gray mist. It was impossible to see from this distance where the stairs led to.

Kit squinted with concentration. The staircase was surrounded by an elaborate network of stones. There were huge holes where stones had once been. What did it all mean?

"The symbols are letters!" he yelled. "That one is a 'Q'. The one next to it is a 'V', I think."

"It's not a 'V', Kit – it's a 'U'," said Izzy slowly. Her brain was racing to solve the puzzle in front of them. "I think that's why the rocks are arranged in fours," she said. "Each set of four stones spells out the word 'QUAD'."

"Something or someone has used it as a code to create a safe path across them," added Kit. "My guess is that we need to make sure we are stepping on all the four letters of the word 'QUAD' to stay safe."

Chapter 4: More Puzzles

The three of them clambered across the stones on all fours, like monkeys. Monk rode on Finn's back, pointing out patterns of letters. They were afraid of stepping on the wrong stone and plummeting into the misty depths beneath them.

Eventually they arrived safely at the bottom o the flight of golden steps. Behind them, the golem roared with fury as he reached the sea of lettered stones. Finn glanced back at it. Would it be able to cross them? They needed to move fast.

They raced up the staircase. At the top was a huge golden tree. In front of it was a hole in the ground. They edged around it carefully. They had reached the tree.

"Something is written on the trunk!" gasped Izzy as they gazed up at it. "Can you see, Kit?"

"I can see the writing," muttered Kit, "but I can't read what it says. The letters all blur together and I can't make out the words."

Finn knew reading had always been a battle for Kit. "I think it's a riddle, Kit," he said. "If I read it, I bet you'll be able to solve it."

The writing had been carved into the ancient tree trunk. Finn traced it gently with his fingers as he read. "I am tall when I am young and short when I am old," he said to Kit. "Can you work out what it means?"

Izzy was looking at a circle of symbols etched into the old tree trunk. "Perhaps one of these is the answer?" she said hopefully.

Kit studied the elaborate images. "I've got it!" he yelled. "It's the candle! A candle melts and gets smaller over time as it burns!"

Behind them the golem was taking a running jump at the lettered tiles. Kit pressed desperately against the image of the candle.

The image shuddered as a hidden mechanism inside the tree cranked into action. The next amber jewel dropped from a secret compartment.

Finn thrust the jewel deep into his pocket. They could not release the spirit from it without the orb. They needed to find the dark spies.

They were now at the top of the flight of steps. "The Misty Steps were created to guard the tree!" murmured Finn. "They lead nowhere!" Beyond the tree was a sheer drop into the mist.

Izzy gasped as she pointed behind them.

The golem was clambering up the steps. It was a terrifying sight. Its body was clumsily formed of uneven and broken rocks, glued together with foul-smelling mud. It was nearly at the top of the steps. There was nowhere left for them to run.

Chapter 5: Trial of the Golem

Finn looked up. The storm that had been threatening all day was drawing closer. Heavy rain clouds jostled for space in the sky above the steps. Finn's mind began to buzz with the start of a plan. "The rain will save us!" he yelled. "We must keep the golem out in the rain!"

The three friends held hands and stood bravely along the top step. The golem lumbered up the last few steps towards them. They held their ground. Monk clung to Finn's neck, his face filled with terror.

It began to rain. Icy water rained down on the golem. Thunder rumbled and lightning crashed around it.

The rain drenched the golem, pounding at the muddy clay that held it together. It was as if its muscles had suddenly turned to jelly. Its huge rocky limbs slipped out of joint as the rain lashed into it. One immense arm crashed down onto

he top step. The slippery stream of mud was
no longer able to hold it to its body.

Consumed with rage, the golem made one
last lunge towards the three friends. It hurled its
collapsing body up onto the top step.

"Run down, NOW!" yelled Finn. The three of
them ran past the golem, racing back down the
stairway behind it.

The rain continued to drum against the golem. It was destroying more and more of the mud holding it together. It was steadily losing control of its body. A huge triangular rock that formed its leg slid away from it. It swayed, then fell through the huge hole in front of the tree. With one last howling roar of defeat, it was gone, into the misty abyss.

They had barely had a chance to draw breath when their next problem appeared over the horizon. The two dark spies were now clambering up the stairway. Their progress was slowed by the heavy rain, but they were getting closer. The storm was still raging around them. Finn cupped his hand round Kit's ear and yelled an urgent plan. Izzy saw Kit's eyes light up.

Then Finn was beside her, shouting the plan into her ear. "Take the amber jewel, Iz!" he yelled. "Stand on the top step! Hold the jewel out to Monk, as if you are passing it to him. Do it now!"

Izzy raced to the top of the flight of steps.
She stood bravely on the very edge of the big
hole in the ground. She held the amber jewel
high up above her head. Even in the swirling mist
and rain, the jewel gave out a bright glow of light.

Chapter 6: Trip Trap!

The spies could not believe their luck. The foolish girl was holding the jewel out to them like a prize! The taller one held the orb, ready to jam the jewel into it. Sniggering greedily, they ran towards Izzy. Their eyes were only on the jewel.

Kit and Finn had been hiding behind some rocks at the top of the steps. Kit's rope was stretched tight between them. As the dark spies took their final step up to the top step, the boys stood up. Keeping the rope pulled taut between them, they pulled it swiftly upwards.

The dark spies had no idea they had stepped into a trap. The rope whipped across their ankles like a grass snake. It tripped them up just as they reached the top step. There was no way they could stop their fall. They dropped through the huge hole in the ground and disappeared into the swirling gray mist.

When Izzy remembered it afterwards, she said

t felt as if that moment was frozen in time. She
saw the greedy glint in the eye of the taller spy
as he reached the top step. Next she saw him
stumble. As he fell, he lost control of the orb held
tightly in his hand. It circled slowly in the air
above his head. Izzy leaped forward and grabbed
it. She caught it just seconds before it disappeared
into the mist forever. She had saved the orb!

The storm was still raging around the three friends as they huddled together on the top step. Izzy was soaked to the bone. She shuddered with cold as she jammed the amber jewel into the orb. Just like that, the storm stopped. The crashing thunder and drenching rain were replaced with a soft golden sunlight. A warm summery breeze blew around the three friends. The murky, gray mist was blown away.

The sudden light reflected off the golden stairway and dazzled Finn. He rubbed his eyes. He felt the presence of the Guardian before he saw him. A huge surge of positive energy surrounded him. Finn watched in amazement as a magnificent hybrid creature stepped out from behind the golden tree.

"The Quadrator," breathed Izzy as she gazed at the next Guardian. The creature bounding into life before them was a quadruped. He was half nimble horse and half noble warrior.

The Quadrator's voice rippled across the air like warm honey. "I sensed there was hope when I felt the land around me shudder," he murmured. "The Guardians owe you a huge debt, Finn. Your bravery will not be forgotten."

Finn took a deep, slow breath. He was still relieved to be alive. Now he was safe and warm.

"Thanks," he said with a grin. "But to be honest, on my own, I'm not worth much." He threw his arms around both of his friends. His voice was breaking with sudden emotion. "As a team, we are able to do things we never thought possible!"

The Quadrator was startled then by an irritated chattering from down near his ankles. Finn bent down. He scooped a disgruntled Monk up in his arms.

"Monk, you are so right!" he laughed. He rubbed the tiny monkey's head affectionately. "We are not a team of three. We are indeed a squad of four!"

Glossary

abyss	–	huge deep space
cluster	–	group of things or people close together
consumed	–	eaten up
cranked	–	made a mechanical movement
disgruntled	–	displeased and sulky
drenching	–	soaking or wetting thoroughly
foolish	–	silly, not sensible
golem	–	mythical figure, artificially created and brought to life, that has no soul
huddled	–	crowded together
jostled	–	bumped against each other
lashed	–	whipped
laxative	–	medicine that relieves constipation
plummeting	–	falling down
sheer	–	going up or down very steeply, almost completely vertical

sniggered   – laughed in a mean or disrespectful way

swirled   – moved along with a whirling motion

taut   – tightly pulled, not slack

toppled   – fell forward

triangular   – three-sided, like a triangle

Ancient Life Along the Nile

by Kathleen Cox

MW01109766

PEARSON

Scott
Foresman

Editorial Offices: Glenview, Illinois • Parsippany, New Jersey • New York, New York
Sales Offices: Needham, Massachusetts • Duluth, Georgia • Glenview, Illinois
Coppell, Texas • Ontario, California • Mesa, Arizona

ISBN: 0-328-13620-4

3 4 5 6 7 8 9 10 V0G1 14 13 12 11 10 09 08 07 06

The Nile River

Thousands of years ago, groups of people who had once been wandering nomads built settlements along the northern end of Africa's Nile River. The Nile is the world's longest river. It flows from the mountains of central Africa north to the Mediterranean Sea. These settlers lived along a six-hundred-mile stretch of land that extended to the Mediterranean coast. Here, the year-round climate was generally mild and dry. Over time, the settlements joined together and formed a series of kingdoms that became the great ancient Egyptian civilization. These kingdoms founded many large cities such as Memphis and Thebes.

Rulers called pharaohs **reigned** over the people of ancient Egypt. The pharaohs owned all the land. They first called themselves servants of the Egyptian gods. Later, they began to think of themselves as gods who lived among the common people. Their subjects accepted this belief and honored the pharaohs, just as they honored the other gods and goddesses in the temples.

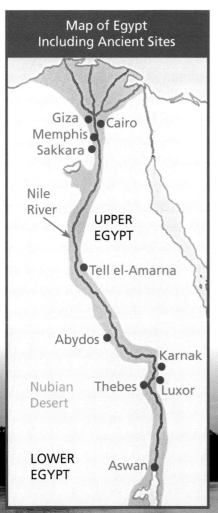

Map of Egypt Including Ancient Sites

Giza
Cairo
Memphis
Sakkara

Nile River

UPPER EGYPT

Tell el-Amarna

Abydos

Karnak

Nubian Desert

Thebes
Luxor

LOWER EGYPT

Aswan

Many cities grew up along the Nile River.

The ancient Egyptians believed that **immortal** gods and goddesses controlled everything that happened in their universe. The gods had power over the movement of the sun, the growth of the people's crops, the success of their hunting and fishing, and the flow of the Nile. The people worshipped their gods and goddesses and hoped that they, in return, would shower the people with good fortune.

Everyone in the kingdom of Egypt worked for the pharaoh. Priests watched over the spiritual well-being of the kingdom. Scribes, who were writers, kept records for the kingdom. They wrote the pharaoh's **decrees,** which informed the citizens of new laws and new taxes. Artists, sculptors, and architects created magnificent structures and artwork, which brought glory to the pharaohs. Other craftsmen shaped soft clay into useful storage containers and pots. Laborers created simple clay homes for the people, boats with delicate papyrus sails, and vast systems of canals that stretched throughout the land.

The Nile River was the center of life in ancient Egypt. Most people in Egypt were farmers. They depended on the river to water the crops that provided most of the harvested food for the kingdom. Other people raised livestock near the Nile. Fishermen brought in the daily catch from the river.

The temple of Ramses II sits on the banks of the Nile River, the center of ancient Egyptian culture.

Another group of citizens provided important services for the people, especially the upper class. Cobblers created leather sandals. Seamstresses and tailors stitched up comfortable clothing to wear in Egypt's warm climate. Jewelers made elaborate adornments out of bronze, gold, and colorful stones. Cooks created meals for the upper classes.

The workers who performed services in the kingdom still depended on the Nile, though not directly. Ancient Egypt did not have money as we know it today. People bartered, or traded, for goods. Cobblers bartered sandals for food. Farmers bartered bags of grain for pottery.

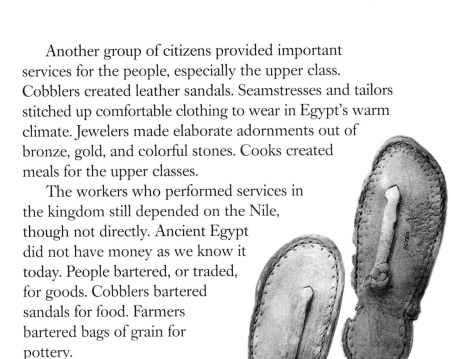

Sandals from ancient Egypt

Writing in Ancient Egypt

Only a very small number of men and women in ancient Egypt knew how to read and write. These people were called scribes. Some scribes were temple priests or administrators who ran the day-to-day activities of the kingdom. Others became architects who helped design the great structures and cities. Scribes worked under the pharaoh and other members of the royalty. They belonged to a very high class.

Scribes were a powerful group of people who could write the hieroglyphic language of Egypt.

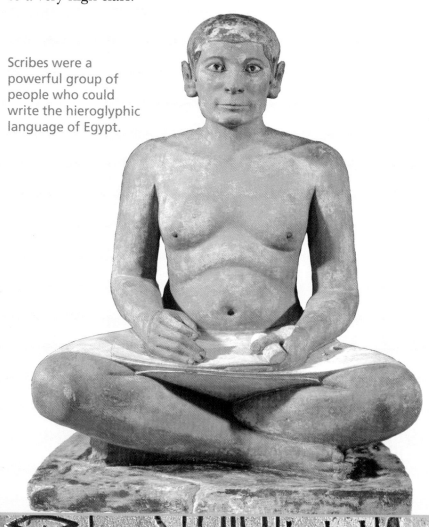

In ancient Egypt, reading and writing meant learning how to read and draw a series of specific pictures. Each picture conveyed an idea or a sound. These picture words are called hieroglyphics. Hieroglyphic writing is one of the oldest systems of writing in the world.

Scribes had to memorize and master the creation of more than seven hundred hieroglyphics. Each picture had to be drawn exactly, or it could be misread. Scribes also studied mathematics and other subjects that were important to the pharaoh and the kingdom.

When scribes wrote hieroglyphic messages, they drew a group of pictures that told a story or conveyed important information. Much of the knowledge we have about daily life in ancient Egypt was actually gathered from hieroglyphics. They have been discovered on the walls of ancient buildings, on tablets, and on **artifacts** such as bits of pottery. Once archaeologists were able to read hieroglyphics, they could solve some of the mysteries of this ancient civilization.

The Nile River provided the tools that scribes used to write their everyday messages as well as the messages that would last for thousands of years. Tablets made from river mud were first used to record hieroglyphics. Later, they used papyrus, a paper-like material made from the papyrus plant. This plant was **abundant** on the banks of the Nile.

To make this paper, the papyrus plant was harvested by laborers. They cut down the stalks, which can grow to be ten feet long, and sliced them into thin strips. Then they soaked the stalks in water for a few days.

Once the water had softened the papyrus stalks, the laborers placed the strips on the ground and pounded them until most of the water drained away. The workers then arranged the strips into large sheets and placed them under boulders. The heavy weight caused the papyrus strips to bond together as they slowly dried out.

Since most people could not read, scribes acted as messengers as well. They would read a royal decree aloud so that citizens could learn about new laws and other decisions made by their pharaoh. This was one important way in which the pharaoh communicated with his subjects and kept them informed.

Papyrus was used for writing and for creating images like this one of a mummy and a spirit.

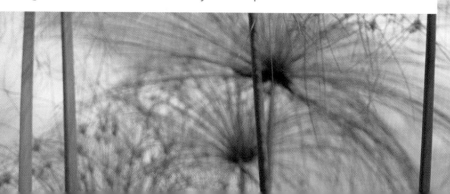

The Nile River was considered the source of life for the ancient Egyptians.

Ancient Egyptian Beliefs

Life for the Egyptians focused on the Nile River, which they believed was at the geographic center of the Earth. They believed that the Earth was flat. They had no way to know otherwise. They didn't have rugged ships that could sail through the rough waves of the oceans, where explorers might discover distant lands that existed beyond their horizon.

The Egyptian people thought that the Earth had started out as mud. They believed that their gods pushed up a mound of solid land called Egypt. The people of Egypt honored their gods for creating their land and the Nile.

Priests and priestesses were responsible for honoring and caring for the gods.

Egyptian priests and priestesses were responsible for making sure that the gods and goddesses were happy. These people were very powerful. If a pharaoh selected a man to become a priest or a woman to become a priestess, then the position would be passed on within the family from generation to generation. A father or mother would pass on the title to a son or daughter. From a young age, the chosen child served under his or her parent and learned the proper rituals and behavior.

All priests followed a strict code of conduct. They kept their bodies clean and pure by taking baths each day in sacred pools. They shaved their heads. They didn't want any of the filth of Earth to pollute their skin or their minds. After all, they were responsible for watching over the spiritual health of the people.

The priests and priestesses organized festivals, took care of the temples, and performed the rituals that marked each important stage of life. The people expected the priests and priestesses to be honorable and to please the gods and goddesses.

To hold their festivals and rituals, the ancient Egyptians built large temples along the Nile. The royal architects designed and supervised the creation of large building projects. Architects also designed the pyramids, which were enormous stone and clay tombs that honored each pharaoh and his family.

Archaeologists believe that the laborers, working under the hot sun for many years, slowly pushed gigantic stones up dirt ramps that were constructed along the walls of the pyramid, until they worked the last stone into place at the top.

The pyramids were so large that it took years to complete just one. The Great Pyramid at Giza is almost five hundred feet tall and covers nearly thirteen acres of land.

Architects and craftsmen also built the Great Sphinx. It was created out of a natural rock formation. Sculptors chiseled the sandstone and slowly shaped it into the head of a pharaoh. Archaeologists are still not sure which pharaoh the Great Sphinx is supposed to represent. The figure wears an ornate headdress and has the body of a lion.

The Great Sphinx is just one of many large structures built by the ancient Egyptians.

Anubis, the god of the dead (at left), stands by at a funeral.

The importance of the Nile carried over into the ancient Egyptian beliefs about the afterlife as well. The Egyptians believed that they should bury their dead on the western side of the great river. The sun set in the west, and they compared the setting sun, which brought an end to the day, to the end of life in this world.

For them, death was a transition. It was a temporary time that signified the end of life in this world and the beginning of life in another world. Because of their belief in an afterlife, the Egyptians took excellent care of their dead. If the dead were mistreated, the Egyptians believed that the spirits of the departed would make life miserable for the relatives who were still alive.

At someone's death, priests took the body and prepared it for its next life. The Egyptians believed that the spirit had already begun its journey to the next world. A priest had to preserve the body. That way, when the body followed the spirit, it would recognize the body and the two would be reunited.

Priests cleaned the body and carefully prepared it for burial. It took forty days to prepare the body. It was then wrapped with strips of linen. Inside the linen wrapping, priests placed amulets and other small treasures to protect the dead person on his or her journey to the afterlife.

The priests covered every inch of the skin with layers of linen to turn the deceased person into a mummy. Then they placed the mummy inside a coffin, which was often carved to look like the deceased.

The family presented the priests with some clothing, food, and other objects that they believed their relative needed for the journey. They wanted the deceased to live well in the hereafter. Some Egyptians asked the priests to include a miniature papyrus boat among the possessions. They believed that their relative would use the small boat to sail on the Nile River to the underworld, where this person would stay for **eternity.**

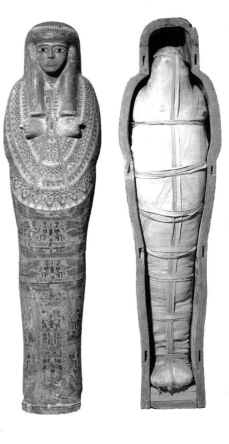

Bodies of the dead were wrapped in linen and stored in coffins.

A funeral barge transported the dead to the afterlife.

The Nile Floods

The Egyptians worshipped the god of the Nile River, Hapi. The river also had a strong influence on their economy. They thought of the river as their refuge from the desert that stretched in every direction. The ancient Egyptian civilization prospered because the Egyptians learned how to live in harmony with the powerful river, which cut through the center of their land.

Egypt receives very little rainfall, so the river water was extremely valuable. But the Nile River was a complicated neighbor. For much of the year it flowed calmly along its northerly course. But after the end of the summer harvest, heavy rains normally fell to the south of the Egyptian kingdom.

The rain-swollen Nile began to rush along its course through the land of ancient Egypt. Eventually, the water spilled over the banks of the river. Floodwaters rushed into the lowlands and covered everything in their path. Because of this seasonal flood, which the Egyptians called the Inundation, the people knew that they needed to build their homes on the highest land in their kingdom. The high elevation usually protected them from the destruction of the late summer flood.

The Egyptians welcomed the Inundation. The floodwaters deposited rich silt from the river onto the dry land. Once the waters **receded,** the silt was exposed and could be used for farming. At other times during the year, farmers had to build canals to get water from the river to their crops.

But sometimes the summer weather and the river didn't cooperate. At times too little summer rain fell to the south. The Nile failed to flow over its banks and saturate the surrounding land. It was difficult to irrigate the newly planted crops. The land dried out and the crops failed.

Sometimes there was too much rain in the summer, and the floodwaters caused terrible destruction. Raging waters washed away homes that were made of hardened clay. The structures simply crumbled and disappeared. Valuable orchards, which took years to establish in the soil, toppled over like flimsy matchsticks.

This picture, taken in the late 1800s, shows the seasonal flooding of the Nile River.

15

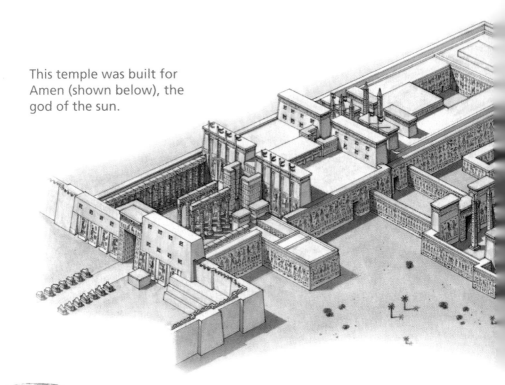

This temple was built for Amen (shown below), the god of the sun.

But when the flood followed its usual pattern, the people of Egypt benefited. They took time to thank their gods and goddesses for their good fortune. During the summer flood, the Egyptians held festivals to honor their gods.

One important festival was the festival of Opet. It honored Amen, the primary sun god, as well as Opet, Mut, and Khons. The festival went on for many days. This was an ideal time for a celebration since people could do very little work. The waters from the Nile River had filled their fields.

People flocked to the city of Karnak to attend the festival, which focused on a colorful procession. Priests removed the statues of the sacred gods from their temples, which were off-limits to common people. The priests put them inside a small shrine and placed the shrine on a small boat attached to poles.

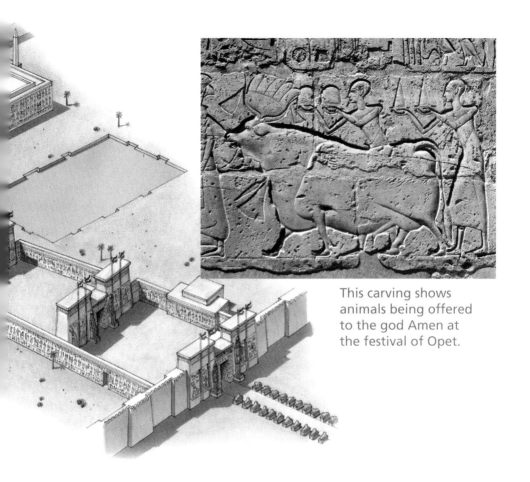

This carving shows animals being offered to the god Amen at the festival of Opet.

The priests balanced the poles on their shoulders. They slowly made their way through narrow streets to a second temple more than a mile away. The people followed close behind. Acrobats thrilled the people with their stunts. Musicians and singers played and sang along the way. The shrine was held high in the air for everyone to see.

When the priests reached the doors that led into the second temple, the pharaoh greeted the sacred statues. People danced. Drums rolled. The priests and the pharaoh took the small shrine with its statues inside the temple, where the pharaoh received divine blessings from the god Amen. Sometimes this entire journey and festival procession took place on boats that floated on the Nile between these two temples.

Farming Along the Nile

When the floodwaters receded from the lowlands, they replenished the farmland by leaving behind a rich coat of silt, or topsoil. This black soil was filled with nutrients such as nitrogen, which enriched the soil. The receding waters signaled the start of the annual season of rebirth and renewal. This was the time for farmers to go into their fields and plant their crops for the next year.

Planting conditions after the flood were perfect. The sun shone brightly, which was necessary for the growth of healthy, strong plants. Many inches of the soil, including the fertile top layer, were extremely muddy from the flood.

The mud made it easier for the farmers to plant their seeds. They didn't have to work a hoe through hard land or struggle to turn over their soil. They didn't have to water their fields once they planted their seeds. The flood did these chores for the farmers.

The farmers grew a wide variety of crops. They planted grains such as barley and wheat. They planted vegetables such as beans, chickpeas, cucumbers, lettuce, and onions. On higher land, the Egyptians created vineyards and orchards. The trees bore fruits such as pomegranates, figs, and dates. The farmers planted gardens of herbs and spices such as dill, thyme, sage, and cumin to flavor their food.

Many ancient Egyptians were farmers or herders.

Many animals were drawn to the Nile River, where they took refuge under the shade of palm trees and drank from the river. Ducks and geese waddled along the riverbanks or swam in the water. Fish, crocodiles, and hippopotamuses also made the river their home. All these creatures were hunted by the Egyptians.

Only the upper class and royalty could afford meals that included meat. The lower classes usually ate vegetarian meals, which they enjoyed with homemade bread. They spiced up their dishes with dill and cumin or sweetened them with honey. They also ate watermelon, grapes, figs, and dates.

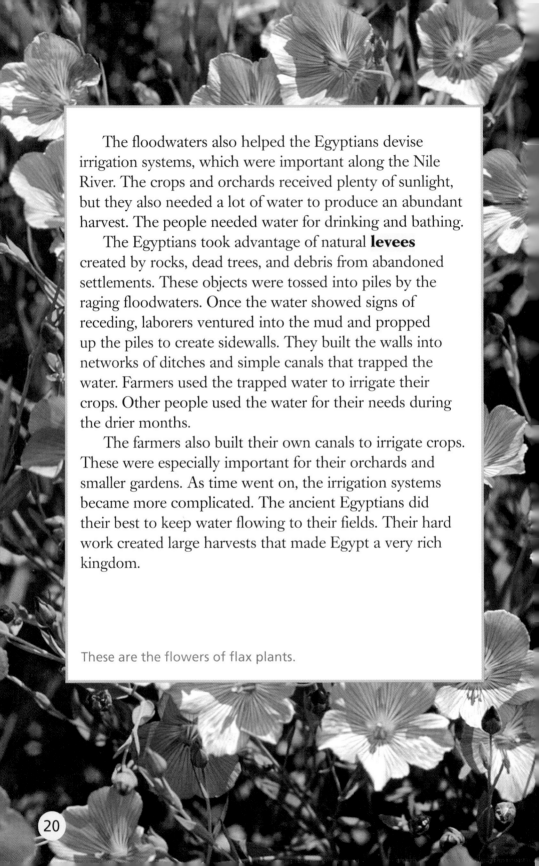

The floodwaters also helped the Egyptians devise irrigation systems, which were important along the Nile River. The crops and orchards received plenty of sunlight, but they also needed a lot of water to produce an abundant harvest. The people needed water for drinking and bathing.

The Egyptians took advantage of natural **levees** created by rocks, dead trees, and debris from abandoned settlements. These objects were tossed into piles by the raging floodwaters. Once the water showed signs of receding, laborers ventured into the mud and propped up the piles to create sidewalls. They built the walls into networks of ditches and simple canals that trapped the water. Farmers used the trapped water to irrigate their crops. Other people used the water for their needs during the drier months.

The farmers also built their own canals to irrigate crops. These were especially important for their orchards and smaller gardens. As time went on, the irrigation systems became more complicated. The ancient Egyptians did their best to keep water flowing to their fields. Their hard work created large harvests that made Egypt a very rich kingdom.

These are the flowers of flax plants.

Many farmers and their families grew flax, which was used to produce linen. Linen was used to make clothing. This important plant was harvested while it was still blooming. Children piled the plants high on their heads. Adults with big bundles stacked in their arms carried the valuable plants from the fields to a flat area where the flax could dry out in the sun. Then women spun the fibers of the flax into thread that was woven into linen.

Ancient flax cord

Clothing was simple and made of linen.

Egyptian Fashion

Clothing in ancient Egypt was relatively simple and functional. Upper-class men usually wore short white skirts, or kilts. Older men wore long comfortable robes that swept down to their ankles.

Upper-class women dressed in close-fitting robes. Sometimes they added a cape-style cloak over their shoulders in the evenings, or if there was a rare cool breeze. The women's hair, jewelry, and elaborate makeup, which was especially dramatic around their eyes, held everyone's attention, not their clothing.

Lower-class men and women wore kilts made of a rougher linen. They were usually midcalf length. This simple attire provided comfort and ease of movement when they worked in the heat or in the fields. Children also wore very simple kilts as they worked beside their parents.

Both sexes cared deeply about their appearance, especially members of the upper class. After they bathed, they dabbed on fragrant oils and creams to protect their skin from the dry heat.

Wealthy men and women spent a good deal of time grooming their hair. They rubbed it with wax from beehives, which held the style and made the hair shine. Many wealthy men and women, including the pharaohs, wore dark wigs designed in elaborate hairstyles.

The people of ancient Egypt loved jewelry. Men and women wore stone-studded metal collars and necklaces that draped down their necks. They wore wide cuffs of bronze, gold, and precious stones around their upper arms, wrists, and ankles. Their fingers sparkled with rings. So did their toes, which would peek out of their leather sandals.

For many centuries the Egyptians retained their customs, from their style of clothing to their religious beliefs. Their kingdom flourished along the Nile River. And for a long time, their civilization prospered.

Egyptians used combs and other objects to be fashionable.

Glossary

abundant *adj.* more than enough; very plentiful.

artifacts *n.* any items made by human skill or work, especially tools or weapons.

decrees *n.* decisions ordered by authority; laws.

eternity *n.* all time; an endless time period.

immortal *adj.* living forever, never dying, everlasting.

levees *n.* high banks built to keep a river from overflowing.

receded *v.* moved backward, withdrew.

reigned *v.* ruled over, as a monarch rules over a nation.

Ancient Life Along the Nile

by Kathleen Cox

Editorial Offices: Glenview, Illinois • Parsippany, New Jersey • New York, New York
Sales Offices: Needham, Massachusetts • Duluth, Georgia • Glenview, Illinois
Coppell, Texas • Ontario, California • Mesa, Arizona

ISBN: 0-328-13620-4

Copyright © Pearson Education, Inc.

3 4 5 6 7 8 9 10 V0G1 14 13 12 11 10 09 08 07 06

The Nile River

Thousands of years ago, groups of people who had once been wandering nomads built settlements along the northern end of Africa's Nile River. The Nile is the world's longest river. It flows from the mountains of central Africa north to the Mediterranean Sea. These settlers lived along a six-hundred-mile stretch of land that extended to the Mediterranean coast. Here, the year-round climate was generally mild and dry. Over time, the settlements joined together and formed a series of kingdoms that became the great ancient Egyptian civilization. These kingdoms founded many large cities such as Memphis and Thebes.

Rulers called pharaohs **reigned** over the people of ancient Egypt. The pharaohs owned all the land. They first called themselves servants of the Egyptian gods. Later, they began to think of themselves as gods who lived among the common people. Their subjects accepted this belief and honored the pharaohs, just as they honored the other gods and goddesses in the temples.

Map of Egypt Including Ancient Sites

Giza
Cairo
Memphis
Sakkara

Nile River

UPPER EGYPT

Tell el-Amarna

Abydos

Karnak

Nubian Desert

Thebes
Luxor

LOWER EGYPT

Aswan

Many cities grew up along the Nile River.

The ancient Egyptians believed that **immortal** gods and goddesses controlled everything that happened in their universe. The gods had power over the movement of the sun, the growth of the people's crops, the success of their hunting and fishing, and the flow of the Nile. The people worshipped their gods and goddesses and hoped that they, in return, would shower the people with good fortune.

Everyone in the kingdom of Egypt worked for the pharaoh. Priests watched over the spiritual well-being of the kingdom. Scribes, who were writers, kept records for the kingdom. They wrote the pharaoh's **decrees,** which informed the citizens of new laws and new taxes. Artists, sculptors, and architects created magnificent structures and artwork, which brought glory to the pharaohs. Other craftsmen shaped soft clay into useful storage containers and pots. Laborers created simple clay homes for the people, boats with delicate papyrus sails, and vast systems of canals that stretched throughout the land.

The Nile River was the center of life in ancient Egypt. Most people in Egypt were farmers. They depended on the river to water the crops that provided most of the harvested food for the kingdom. Other people raised livestock near the Nile. Fishermen brought in the daily catch from the river.

The temple of Ramses II sits on the banks of the Nile River, the center of ancient Egyptian culture.

Another group of citizens provided important services for the people, especially the upper class. Cobblers created leather sandals. Seamstresses and tailors stitched up comfortable clothing to wear in Egypt's warm climate. Jewelers made elaborate adornments out of bronze, gold, and colorful stones. Cooks created meals for the upper classes.

The workers who performed services in the kingdom still depended on the Nile, though not directly. Ancient Egypt did not have money as we know it today. People bartered, or traded, for goods. Cobblers bartered sandals for food. Farmers bartered bags of grain for pottery.

Sandals from ancient Egypt

Writing in Ancient Egypt

Only a very small number of men and women in ancient Egypt knew how to read and write. These people were called scribes. Some scribes were temple priests or administrators who ran the day-to-day activities of the kingdom. Others became architects who helped design the great structures and cities. Scribes worked under the pharaoh and other members of the royalty. They belonged to a very high class.

Scribes were a powerful group of people who could write the hieroglyphic language of Egypt.

In ancient Egypt, reading and writing meant learning how to read and draw a series of specific pictures. Each picture conveyed an idea or a sound. These picture words are called hieroglyphics. Hieroglyphic writing is one of the oldest systems of writing in the world.

Scribes had to memorize and master the creation of more than seven hundred hieroglyphics. Each picture had to be drawn exactly, or it could be misread. Scribes also studied mathematics and other subjects that were important to the pharaoh and the kingdom.

When scribes wrote hieroglyphic messages, they drew a group of pictures that told a story or conveyed important information. Much of the knowledge we have about daily life in ancient Egypt was actually gathered from hieroglyphics. They have been discovered on the walls of ancient buildings, on tablets, and on **artifacts** such as bits of pottery. Once archaeologists were able to read hieroglyphics, they could solve some of the mysteries of this ancient civilization.

The Nile River provided the tools that scribes used to write their everyday messages as well as the messages that would last for thousands of years. Tablets made from river mud were first used to record hieroglyphics. Later, they used papyrus, a paper-like material made from the papyrus plant. This plant was **abundant** on the banks of the Nile.

To make this paper, the papyrus plant was harvested by laborers. They cut down the stalks, which can grow to be ten feet long, and sliced them into thin strips. Then they soaked the stalks in water for a few days.

Once the water had softened the papyrus stalks, the laborers placed the strips on the ground and pounded them until most of the water drained away. The workers then arranged the strips into large sheets and placed them under boulders. The heavy weight caused the papyrus strips to bond together as they slowly dried out.

Since most people could not read, scribes acted as messengers as well. They would read a royal decree aloud so that citizens could learn about new laws and other decisions made by their pharaoh. This was one important way in which the pharaoh communicated with his subjects and kept them informed.

Papyrus was used for writing and for creating images like this one of a mummy and a spirit.

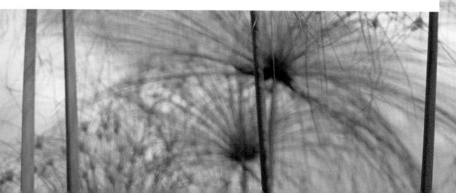

The Nile River was considered the source of life for the ancient Egyptians.

Ancient Egyptian Beliefs

Life for the Egyptians focused on the Nile River, which they believed was at the geographic center of the Earth. They believed that the Earth was flat. They had no way to know otherwise. They didn't have rugged ships that could sail through the rough waves of the oceans, where explorers might discover distant lands that existed beyond their horizon.

The Egyptian people thought that the Earth had started out as mud. They believed that their gods pushed up a mound of solid land called Egypt. The people of Egypt honored their gods for creating their land and the Nile.

Priests and priestesses were responsible for honoring and caring for the gods.

Egyptian priests and priestesses were responsible for making sure that the gods and goddesses were happy. These people were very powerful. If a pharaoh selected a man to become a priest or a woman to become a priestess, then the position would be passed on within the family from generation to generation. A father or mother would pass on the title to a son or daughter. From a young age, the chosen child served under his or her parent and learned the proper rituals and behavior.

All priests followed a strict code of conduct. They kept their bodies clean and pure by taking baths each day in sacred pools. They shaved their heads. They didn't want any of the filth of Earth to pollute their skin or their minds. After all, they were responsible for watching over the spiritual health of the people.

The priests and priestesses organized festivals, took care of the temples, and performed the rituals that marked each important stage of life. The people expected the priests and priestesses to be honorable and to please the gods and goddesses.

To hold their festivals and rituals, the ancient Egyptians built large temples along the Nile. The royal architects designed and supervised the creation of large building projects. Architects also designed the pyramids, which were enormous stone and clay tombs that honored each pharaoh and his family.

Archaeologists believe that the laborers, working under the hot sun for many years, slowly pushed gigantic stones up dirt ramps that were constructed along the walls of the pyramid, until they worked the last stone into place at the top.

The pyramids were so large that it took years to complete just one. The Great Pyramid at Giza is almost five hundred feet tall and covers nearly thirteen acres of land.

Architects and craftsmen also built the Great Sphinx. It was created out of a natural rock formation. Sculptors chiseled the sandstone and slowly shaped it into the head of a pharaoh. Archaeologists are still not sure which pharaoh the Great Sphinx is supposed to represent. The figure wears an ornate headdress and has the body of a lion.

The Great Sphinx is just one of many large structures built by the ancient Egyptians.

Anubis, the god of the dead (at left), stands by at a funeral.

The importance of the Nile carried over into the ancient Egyptian beliefs about the afterlife as well. The Egyptians believed that they should bury their dead on the western side of the great river. The sun set in the west, and they compared the setting sun, which brought an end to the day, to the end of life in this world.

For them, death was a transition. It was a temporary time that signified the end of life in this world and the beginning of life in another world. Because of their belief in an afterlife, the Egyptians took excellent care of their dead. If the dead were mistreated, the Egyptians believed that the spirits of the departed would make life miserable for the relatives who were still alive.

At someone's death, priests took the body and prepared it for its next life. The Egyptians believed that the spirit had already begun its journey to the next world. A priest had to preserve the body. That way, when the body followed the spirit, it would recognize the body and the two would be reunited.

Priests cleaned the body and carefully prepared it for burial. It took forty days to prepare the body. It was then wrapped with strips of linen. Inside the linen wrapping, priests placed amulets and other small treasures to protect the dead person on his or her journey to the afterlife.

The priests covered every inch of the skin with layers of linen to turn the deceased person into a mummy. Then they placed the mummy inside a coffin, which was often carved to look like the deceased.

The family presented the priests with some clothing, food, and other objects that they believed their relative needed for the journey. They wanted the deceased to live well in the hereafter. Some Egyptians asked the priests to include a miniature papyrus boat among the possessions. They believed that their relative would use the small boat to sail on the Nile River to the underworld, where this person would stay for **eternity.**

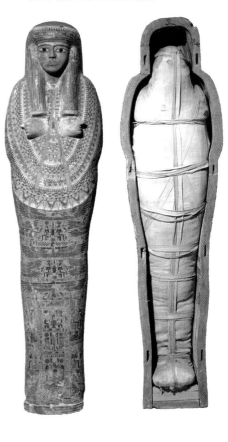

Bodies of the dead were wrapped in linen and stored in coffins.

A funeral barge transported the dead to the afterlife.

The Nile Floods

The Egyptians worshipped the god of the Nile River, Hapi. The river also had a strong influence on their economy. They thought of the river as their refuge from the desert that stretched in every direction. The ancient Egyptian civilization prospered because the Egyptians learned how to live in harmony with the powerful river, which cut through the center of their land.

Egypt receives very little rainfall, so the river water was extremely valuable. But the Nile River was a complicated neighbor. For much of the year it flowed calmly along its northerly course. But after the end of the summer harvest, heavy rains normally fell to the south of the Egyptian kingdom.

The rain-swollen Nile began to rush along its course through the land of ancient Egypt. Eventually, the water spilled over the banks of the river. Floodwaters rushed into the lowlands and covered everything in their path. Because of this seasonal flood, which the Egyptians called the Inundation, the people knew that they needed to build their homes on the highest land in their kingdom. The high elevation usually protected them from the destruction of the late summer flood.

The Egyptians welcomed the Inundation. The floodwaters deposited rich silt from the river onto the dry land. Once the waters **receded,** the silt was exposed and could be used for farming. At other times during the year, farmers had to build canals to get water from the river to their crops.

But sometimes the summer weather and the river didn't cooperate. At times too little summer rain fell to the south. The Nile failed to flow over its banks and saturate the surrounding land. It was difficult to irrigate the newly planted crops. The land dried out and the crops failed.

Sometimes there was too much rain in the summer, and the floodwaters caused terrible destruction. Raging waters washed away homes that were made of hardened clay. The structures simply crumbled and disappeared. Valuable orchards, which took years to establish in the soil, toppled over like flimsy matchsticks.

This picture, taken in the late 1800s, shows the seasonal flooding of the Nile River.

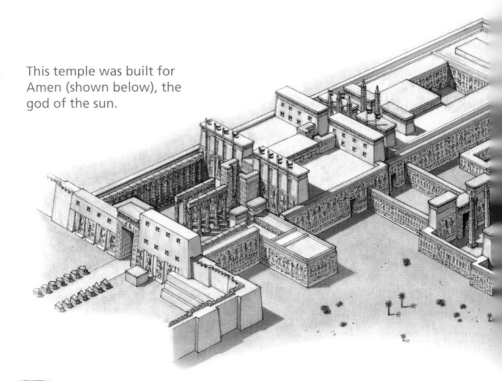

This temple was built for Amen (shown below), the god of the sun.

But when the flood followed its usual pattern, the people of Egypt benefited. They took time to thank their gods and goddesses for their good fortune. During the summer flood, the Egyptians held festivals to honor their gods.

One important festival was the festival of Opet. It honored Amen, the primary sun god, as well as Opet, Mut, and Khons. The festival went on for many days. This was an ideal time for a celebration since people could do very little work. The waters from the Nile River had filled their fields.

People flocked to the city of Karnak to attend the festival, which focused on a colorful procession. Priests removed the statues of the sacred gods from their temples, which were off-limits to common people. The priests put them inside a small shrine and placed the shrine on a small boat attached to poles.

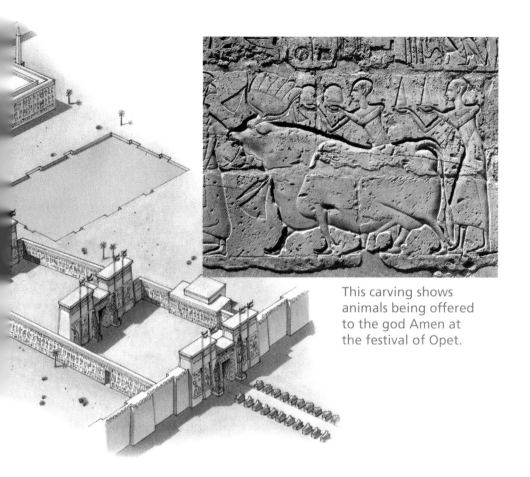

This carving shows animals being offered to the god Amen at the festival of Opet.

The priests balanced the poles on their shoulders. They slowly made their way through narrow streets to a second temple more than a mile away. The people followed close behind. Acrobats thrilled the people with their stunts. Musicians and singers played and sang along the way. The shrine was held high in the air for everyone to see.

When the priests reached the doors that led into the second temple, the pharaoh greeted the sacred statues. People danced. Drums rolled. The priests and the pharaoh took the small shrine with its statues inside the temple, where the pharaoh received divine blessings from the god Amen. Sometimes this entire journey and festival procession took place on boats that floated on the Nile between these two temples.

Farming Along the Nile

When the floodwaters receded from the lowlands, they replenished the farmland by leaving behind a rich coat of silt, or topsoil. This black soil was filled with nutrients such as nitrogen, which enriched the soil. The receding waters signaled the start of the annual season of rebirth and renewal. This was the time for farmers to go into their fields and plant their crops for the next year.

Planting conditions after the flood were perfect. The sun shone brightly, which was necessary for the growth of healthy, strong plants. Many inches of the soil, including the fertile top layer, were extremely muddy from the flood.

The mud made it easier for the farmers to plant their seeds. They didn't have to work a hoe through hard land or struggle to turn over their soil. They didn't have to water their fields once they planted their seeds. The flood did these chores for the farmers.

The farmers grew a wide variety of crops. They planted grains such as barley and wheat. They planted vegetables such as beans, chickpeas, cucumbers, lettuce, and onions. On higher land, the Egyptians created vineyards and orchards. The trees bore fruits such as pomegranates, figs, and dates. The farmers planted gardens of herbs and spices such as dill, thyme, sage, and cumin to flavor their food.

Many ancient Egyptians were farmers or herders.

Many animals were drawn to the Nile River, where they took refuge under the shade of palm trees and drank from the river. Ducks and geese waddled along the riverbanks or swam in the water. Fish, crocodiles, and hippopotamuses also made the river their home. All these creatures were hunted by the Egyptians.

Only the upper class and royalty could afford meals that included meat. The lower classes usually ate vegetarian meals, which they enjoyed with homemade bread. They spiced up their dishes with dill and cumin or sweetened them with honey. They also ate watermelon, grapes, figs, and dates.

The floodwaters also helped the Egyptians devise irrigation systems, which were important along the Nile River. The crops and orchards received plenty of sunlight, but they also needed a lot of water to produce an abundant harvest. The people needed water for drinking and bathing.

The Egyptians took advantage of natural **levees** created by rocks, dead trees, and debris from abandoned settlements. These objects were tossed into piles by the raging floodwaters. Once the water showed signs of receding, laborers ventured into the mud and propped up the piles to create sidewalls. They built the walls into networks of ditches and simple canals that trapped the water. Farmers used the trapped water to irrigate their crops. Other people used the water for their needs during the drier months.

The farmers also built their own canals to irrigate crops. These were especially important for their orchards and smaller gardens. As time went on, the irrigation systems became more complicated. The ancient Egyptians did their best to keep water flowing to their fields. Their hard work created large harvests that made Egypt a very rich kingdom.

These are the flowers of flax plants.

Many farmers and their families grew flax, which was used to produce linen. Linen was used to make clothing. This important plant was harvested while it was still blooming. Children piled the plants high on their heads. Adults with big bundles stacked in their arms carried the valuable plants from the fields to a flat area where the flax could dry out in the sun. Then women spun the fibers of the flax into thread that was woven into linen.

Ancient flax cord

Clothing was simple and made of linen.

Egyptian Fashion

Clothing in ancient Egypt was relatively simple and functional. Upper-class men usually wore short white skirts, or kilts. Older men wore long comfortable robes that swept down to their ankles.

Upper-class women dressed in close-fitting robes. Sometimes they added a cape-style cloak over their shoulders in the evenings, or if there was a rare cool breeze. The women's hair, jewelry, and elaborate makeup, which was especially dramatic around their eyes, held everyone's attention, not their clothing.

Lower-class men and women wore kilts made of a rougher linen. They were usually midcalf length. This simple attire provided comfort and ease of movement when they worked in the heat or in the fields. Children also wore very simple kilts as they worked beside their parents.

Both sexes cared deeply about their appearance, especially members of the upper class. After they bathed, they dabbed on fragrant oils and creams to protect their skin from the dry heat.

Wealthy men and women spent a good deal of time grooming their hair. They rubbed it with wax from beehives, which held the style and made the hair shine. Many wealthy men and women, including the pharaohs, wore dark wigs designed in elaborate hairstyles.

The people of ancient Egypt loved jewelry. Men and women wore stone-studded metal collars and necklaces that draped down their necks. They wore wide cuffs of bronze, gold, and precious stones around their upper arms, wrists, and ankles. Their fingers sparkled with rings. So did their toes, which would peek out of their leather sandals.

For many centuries the Egyptians retained their customs, from their style of clothing to their religious beliefs. Their kingdom flourished along the Nile River. And for a long time, their civilization prospered.

Egyptians used combs and other objects to be fashionable.

Glossary

abundant *adj.* more than enough; very plentiful.

artifacts *n.* any items made by human skill or work, especially tools or weapons.

decrees *n.* decisions ordered by authority; laws.

eternity *n.* all time; an endless time period.

immortal *adj.* living forever, never dying, everlasting.

levees *n.* high banks built to keep a river from overflowing.

receded *v.* moved backward, withdrew.

reigned *v.* ruled over, as a monarch rules over a nation.

Ancient Life Along the Nile

by Kathleen Cox

PEARSON

Scott
Foresman

Editorial Offices: Glenview, Illinois • Parsippany, New Jersey • New York, New York
Sales Offices: Needham, Massachusetts • Duluth, Georgia • Glenview, Illinois
Coppell, Texas • Ontario, California • Mesa, Arizona

ISBN: 0-328-13620-4

3 4 5 6 7 8 9 10 V0G1 14 13 12 11 10 09 08 07 06

The Nile River

Thousands of years ago, groups of people who had once been wandering nomads built settlements along the northern end of Africa's Nile River. The Nile is the world's longest river. It flows from the mountains of central Africa north to the Mediterranean Sea. These settlers lived along a six-hundred-mile stretch of land that extended to the Mediterranean coast. Here, the year-round climate was generally mild and dry. Over time, the settlements joined together and formed a series of kingdoms that became the great ancient Egyptian civilization. These kingdoms founded many large cities such as Memphis and Thebes.

Rulers called pharaohs **reigned** over the people of ancient Egypt. The pharaohs owned all the land. They first called themselves servants of the Egyptian gods. Later, they began to think of themselves as gods who lived among the common people. Their subjects accepted this belief and honored the pharaohs, just as they honored the other gods and goddesses in the temples.

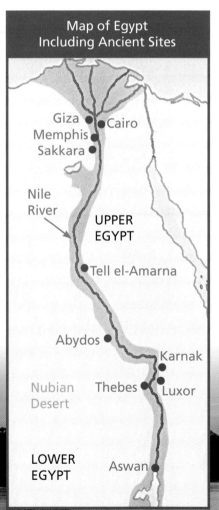

Map of Egypt Including Ancient Sites

Giza
Cairo
Memphis
Sakkara

Nile River

UPPER EGYPT

Tell el-Amarna

Abydos

Karnak

Nubian Desert

Thebes
Luxor

LOWER EGYPT

Aswan

Many cities grew up along the Nile River.

The ancient Egyptians believed that **immortal** gods and goddesses controlled everything that happened in their universe. The gods had power over the movement of the sun, the growth of the people's crops, the success of their hunting and fishing, and the flow of the Nile. The people worshipped their gods and goddesses and hoped that they, in return, would shower the people with good fortune.

Everyone in the kingdom of Egypt worked for the pharaoh. Priests watched over the spiritual well-being of the kingdom. Scribes, who were writers, kept records for the kingdom. They wrote the pharaoh's **decrees,** which informed the citizens of new laws and new taxes. Artists, sculptors, and architects created magnificent structures and artwork, which brought glory to the pharaohs. Other craftsmen shaped soft clay into useful storage containers and pots. Laborers created simple clay homes for the people, boats with delicate papyrus sails, and vast systems of canals that stretched throughout the land.

The Nile River was the center of life in ancient Egypt. Most people in Egypt were farmers. They depended on the river to water the crops that provided most of the harvested food for the kingdom. Other people raised livestock near the Nile. Fishermen brought in the daily catch from the river.

The temple of Ramses II sits on the banks of the Nile River, the center of ancient Egyptian culture.

Another group of citizens provided important services for the people, especially the upper class. Cobblers created leather sandals. Seamstresses and tailors stitched up comfortable clothing to wear in Egypt's warm climate. Jewelers made elaborate adornments out of bronze, gold, and colorful stones. Cooks created meals for the upper classes.

The workers who performed services in the kingdom still depended on the Nile, though not directly. Ancient Egypt did not have money as we know it today. People bartered, or traded, for goods. Cobblers bartered sandals for food. Farmers bartered bags of grain for pottery.

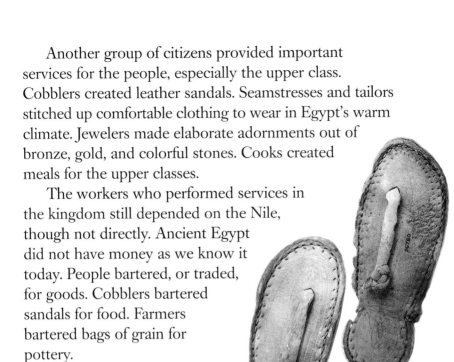

Sandals from ancient Egypt

Writing in Ancient Egypt

Only a very small number of men and women in ancient Egypt knew how to read and write. These people were called scribes. Some scribes were temple priests or administrators who ran the day-to-day activities of the kingdom. Others became architects who helped design the great structures and cities. Scribes worked under the pharaoh and other members of the royalty. They belonged to a very high class.

Scribes were a powerful group of people who could write the hieroglyphic language of Egypt.

In ancient Egypt, reading and writing meant learning how to read and draw a series of specific pictures. Each picture conveyed an idea or a sound. These picture words are called hieroglyphics. Hieroglyphic writing is one of the oldest systems of writing in the world.

Scribes had to memorize and master the creation of more than seven hundred hieroglyphics. Each picture had to be drawn exactly, or it could be misread. Scribes also studied mathematics and other subjects that were important to the pharaoh and the kingdom.

When scribes wrote hieroglyphic messages, they drew a group of pictures that told a story or conveyed important information. Much of the knowledge we have about daily life in ancient Egypt was actually gathered from hieroglyphics. They have been discovered on the walls of ancient buildings, on tablets, and on **artifacts** such as bits of pottery. Once archaeologists were able to read hieroglyphics, they could solve some of the mysteries of this ancient civilization.

The Nile River provided the tools that scribes used to write their everyday messages as well as the messages that would last for thousands of years. Tablets made from river mud were first used to record hieroglyphics. Later, they used papyrus, a paper-like material made from the papyrus plant. This plant was **abundant** on the banks of the Nile.

To make this paper, the papyrus plant was harvested by laborers. They cut down the stalks, which can grow to be ten feet long, and sliced them into thin strips. Then they soaked the stalks in water for a few days.

Once the water had softened the papyrus stalks, the laborers placed the strips on the ground and pounded them until most of the water drained away. The workers then arranged the strips into large sheets and placed them under boulders. The heavy weight caused the papyrus strips to bond together as they slowly dried out.

Since most people could not read, scribes acted as messengers as well. They would read a royal decree aloud so that citizens could learn about new laws and other decisions made by their pharaoh. This was one important way in which the pharaoh communicated with his subjects and kept them informed.

Papyrus was used for writing and for creating images like this one of a mummy and a spirit.

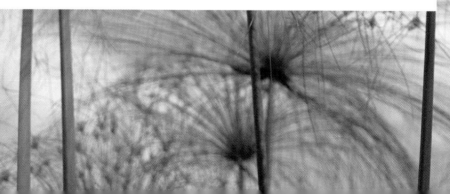

The Nile River was considered the source of life for the ancient Egyptians.

Ancient Egyptian Beliefs

Life for the Egyptians focused on the Nile River, which they believed was at the geographic center of the Earth. They believed that the Earth was flat. They had no way to know otherwise. They didn't have rugged ships that could sail through the rough waves of the oceans, where explorers might discover distant lands that existed beyond their horizon.

The Egyptian people thought that the Earth had started out as mud. They believed that their gods pushed up a mound of solid land called Egypt. The people of Egypt honored their gods for creating their land and the Nile.

Priests and priestesses were responsible for honoring and caring for the gods.

Egyptian priests and priestesses were responsible for making sure that the gods and goddesses were happy. These people were very powerful. If a pharaoh selected a man to become a priest or a woman to become a priestess, then the position would be passed on within the family from generation to generation. A father or mother would pass on the title to a son or daughter. From a young age, the chosen child served under his or her parent and learned the proper rituals and behavior.

All priests followed a strict code of conduct. They kept their bodies clean and pure by taking baths each day in sacred pools. They shaved their heads. They didn't want any of the filth of Earth to pollute their skin or their minds. After all, they were responsible for watching over the spiritual health of the people.

The priests and priestesses organized festivals, took care of the temples, and performed the rituals that marked each important stage of life. The people expected the priests and priestesses to be honorable and to please the gods and goddesses.

To hold their festivals and rituals, the ancient Egyptians built large temples along the Nile. The royal architects designed and supervised the creation of large building projects. Architects also designed the pyramids, which were enormous stone and clay tombs that honored each pharaoh and his family.

Archaeologists believe that the laborers, working under the hot sun for many years, slowly pushed gigantic stones up dirt ramps that were constructed along the walls of the pyramid, until they worked the last stone into place at the top.

The pyramids were so large that it took years to complete just one. The Great Pyramid at Giza is almost five hundred feet tall and covers nearly thirteen acres of land.

Architects and craftsmen also built the Great Sphinx. It was created out of a natural rock formation. Sculptors chiseled the sandstone and slowly shaped it into the head of a pharaoh. Archaeologists are still not sure which pharaoh the Great Sphinx is supposed to represent. The figure wears an ornate headdress and has the body of a lion.

The Great Sphinx is just one of many large structures built by the ancient Egyptians.

Anubis, the god of the dead (at left), stands by at a funeral.

The importance of the Nile carried over into the ancient Egyptian beliefs about the afterlife as well. The Egyptians believed that they should bury their dead on the western side of the great river. The sun set in the west, and they compared the setting sun, which brought an end to the day, to the end of life in this world.

For them, death was a transition. It was a temporary time that signified the end of life in this world and the beginning of life in another world. Because of their belief in an afterlife, the Egyptians took excellent care of their dead. If the dead were mistreated, the Egyptians believed that the spirits of the departed would make life miserable for the relatives who were still alive.

At someone's death, priests took the body and prepared it for its next life. The Egyptians believed that the spirit had already begun its journey to the next world. A priest had to preserve the body. That way, when the body followed the spirit, it would recognize the body and the two would be reunited.

Priests cleaned the body and carefully prepared it for burial. It took forty days to prepare the body. It was then wrapped with strips of linen. Inside the linen wrapping, priests placed amulets and other small treasures to protect the dead person on his or her journey to the afterlife.

The priests covered every inch of the skin with layers of linen to turn the deceased person into a mummy. Then they placed the mummy inside a coffin, which was often carved to look like the deceased.

The family presented the priests with some clothing, food, and other objects that they believed their relative needed for the journey. They wanted the deceased to live well in the hereafter. Some Egyptians asked the priests to include a miniature papyrus boat among the possessions. They believed that their relative would use the small boat to sail on the Nile River to the underworld, where this person would stay for **eternity.**

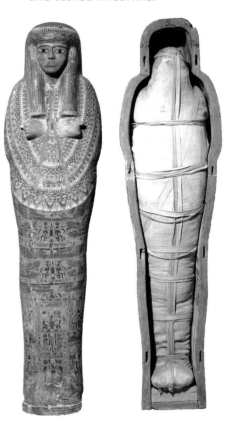

Bodies of the dead were wrapped in linen and stored in coffins.

A funeral barge transported the dead to the afterlife.

The Nile Floods

The Egyptians worshipped the god of the Nile River, Hapi. The river also had a strong influence on their economy. They thought of the river as their refuge from the desert that stretched in every direction. The ancient Egyptian civilization prospered because the Egyptians learned how to live in harmony with the powerful river, which cut through the center of their land.

Egypt receives very little rainfall, so the river water was extremely valuable. But the Nile River was a complicated neighbor. For much of the year it flowed calmly along its northerly course. But after the end of the summer harvest, heavy rains normally fell to the south of the Egyptian kingdom.

The rain-swollen Nile began to rush along its course through the land of ancient Egypt. Eventually, the water spilled over the banks of the river. Floodwaters rushed into the lowlands and covered everything in their path. Because of this seasonal flood, which the Egyptians called the Inundation, the people knew that they needed to build their homes on the highest land in their kingdom. The high elevation usually protected them from the destruction of the late summer flood.

The Egyptians welcomed the Inundation. The floodwaters deposited rich silt from the river onto the dry land. Once the waters **receded,** the silt was exposed and could be used for farming. At other times during the year, farmers had to build canals to get water from the river to their crops.

But sometimes the summer weather and the river didn't cooperate. At times too little summer rain fell to the south. The Nile failed to flow over its banks and saturate the surrounding land. It was difficult to irrigate the newly planted crops. The land dried out and the crops failed.

Sometimes there was too much rain in the summer, and the floodwaters caused terrible destruction. Raging waters washed away homes that were made of hardened clay. The structures simply crumbled and disappeared. Valuable orchards, which took years to establish in the soil, toppled over like flimsy matchsticks.

This picture, taken in the late 1800s, shows the seasonal flooding of the Nile River.

15

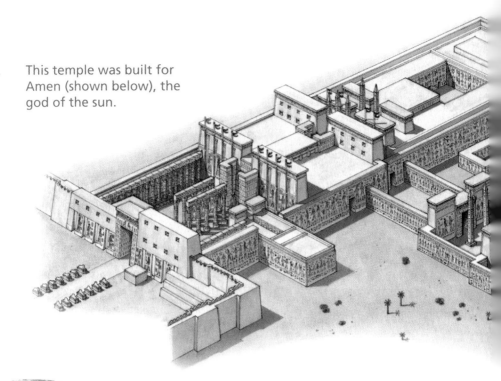

This temple was built for Amen (shown below), the god of the sun.

But when the flood followed its usual pattern, the people of Egypt benefited. They took time to thank their gods and goddesses for their good fortune. During the summer flood, the Egyptians held festivals to honor their gods.

One important festival was the festival of Opet. It honored Amen, the primary sun god, as well as Opet, Mut, and Khons. The festival went on for many days. This was an ideal time for a celebration since people could do very little work. The waters from the Nile River had filled their fields.

People flocked to the city of Karnak to attend the festival, which focused on a colorful procession. Priests removed the statues of the sacred gods from their temples, which were off-limits to common people. The priests put them inside a small shrine and placed the shrine on a small boat attached to poles.

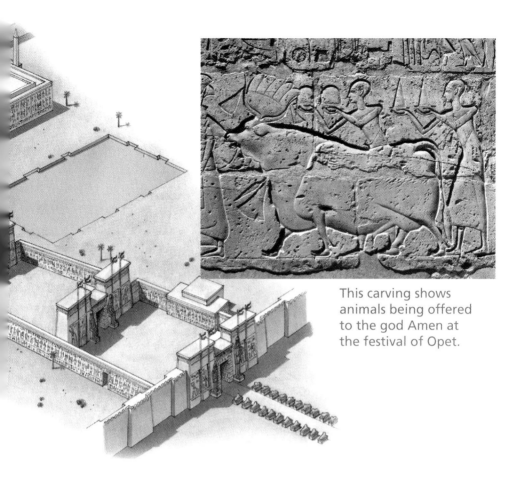

This carving shows animals being offered to the god Amen at the festival of Opet.

The priests balanced the poles on their shoulders. They slowly made their way through narrow streets to a second temple more than a mile away. The people followed close behind. Acrobats thrilled the people with their stunts. Musicians and singers played and sang along the way. The shrine was held high in the air for everyone to see.

When the priests reached the doors that led into the second temple, the pharaoh greeted the sacred statues. People danced. Drums rolled. The priests and the pharaoh took the small shrine with its statues inside the temple, where the pharaoh received divine blessings from the god Amen. Sometimes this entire journey and festival procession took place on boats that floated on the Nile between these two temples.

Farming Along the Nile

When the floodwaters receded from the lowlands, they replenished the farmland by leaving behind a rich coat of silt, or topsoil. This black soil was filled with nutrients such as nitrogen, which enriched the soil. The receding waters signaled the start of the annual season of rebirth and renewal. This was the time for farmers to go into their fields and plant their crops for the next year.

Planting conditions after the flood were perfect. The sun shone brightly, which was necessary for the growth of healthy, strong plants. Many inches of the soil, including the fertile top layer, were extremely muddy from the flood.

The mud made it easier for the farmers to plant their seeds. They didn't have to work a hoe through hard land or struggle to turn over their soil. They didn't have to water their fields once they planted their seeds. The flood did these chores for the farmers.

The farmers grew a wide variety of crops. They planted grains such as barley and wheat. They planted vegetables such as beans, chickpeas, cucumbers, lettuce, and onions. On higher land, the Egyptians created vineyards and orchards. The trees bore fruits such as pomegranates, figs, and dates. The farmers planted gardens of herbs and spices such as dill, thyme, sage, and cumin to flavor their food.

Many ancient Egyptians were farmers or herders.

Many animals were drawn to the Nile River, where they took refuge under the shade of palm trees and drank from the river. Ducks and geese waddled along the riverbanks or swam in the water. Fish, crocodiles, and hippopotamuses also made the river their home. All these creatures were hunted by the Egyptians.

Only the upper class and royalty could afford meals that included meat. The lower classes usually ate vegetarian meals, which they enjoyed with homemade bread. They spiced up their dishes with dill and cumin or sweetened them with honey. They also ate watermelon, grapes, figs, and dates.

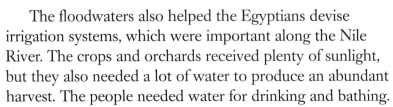

The floodwaters also helped the Egyptians devise irrigation systems, which were important along the Nile River. The crops and orchards received plenty of sunlight, but they also needed a lot of water to produce an abundant harvest. The people needed water for drinking and bathing.

The Egyptians took advantage of natural **levees** created by rocks, dead trees, and debris from abandoned settlements. These objects were tossed into piles by the raging floodwaters. Once the water showed signs of receding, laborers ventured into the mud and propped up the piles to create sidewalls. They built the walls into networks of ditches and simple canals that trapped the water. Farmers used the trapped water to irrigate their crops. Other people used the water for their needs during the drier months.

The farmers also built their own canals to irrigate crops. These were especially important for their orchards and smaller gardens. As time went on, the irrigation systems became more complicated. The ancient Egyptians did their best to keep water flowing to their fields. Their hard work created large harvests that made Egypt a very rich kingdom.

These are the flowers of flax plants.

Many farmers and their families grew flax, which was used to produce linen. Linen was used to make clothing. This important plant was harvested while it was still blooming. Children piled the plants high on their heads. Adults with big bundles stacked in their arms carried the valuable plants from the fields to a flat area where the flax could dry out in the sun. Then women spun the fibers of the flax into thread that was woven into linen.

Ancient flax cord

Clothing was simple and made of linen.

Egyptian Fashion

Clothing in ancient Egypt was relatively simple and functional. Upper-class men usually wore short white skirts, or kilts. Older men wore long comfortable robes that swept down to their ankles.

Upper-class women dressed in close-fitting robes. Sometimes they added a cape-style cloak over their shoulders in the evenings, or if there was a rare cool breeze. The women's hair, jewelry, and elaborate makeup, which was especially dramatic around their eyes, held everyone's attention, not their clothing.

Lower-class men and women wore kilts made of a rougher linen. They were usually midcalf length. This simple attire provided comfort and ease of movement when they worked in the heat or in the fields. Children also wore very simple kilts as they worked beside their parents.

Both sexes cared deeply about their appearance, especially members of the upper class. After they bathed, they dabbed on fragrant oils and creams to protect their skin from the dry heat.

Wealthy men and women spent a good deal of time grooming their hair. They rubbed it with wax from beehives, which held the style and made the hair shine. Many wealthy men and women, including the pharaohs, wore dark wigs designed in elaborate hairstyles.

The people of ancient Egypt loved jewelry. Men and women wore stone-studded metal collars and necklaces that draped down their necks. They wore wide cuffs of bronze, gold, and precious stones around their upper arms, wrists, and ankles. Their fingers sparkled with rings. So did their toes, which would peek out of their leather sandals.

For many centuries the Egyptians retained their customs, from their style of clothing to their religious beliefs. Their kingdom flourished along the Nile River. And for a long time, their civilization prospered.

Egyptians used combs and other objects to be fashionable.

Glossary

abundant *adj.* more than enough; very plentiful.

artifacts *n.* any items made by human skill or work, especially tools or weapons.

decrees *n.* decisions ordered by authority; laws.

eternity *n.* all time; an endless time period.

immortal *adj.* living forever, never dying, everlasting.

levees *n.* high banks built to keep a river from overflowing.

receded *v.* moved backward, withdrew.

reigned *v.* ruled over, as a monarch rules over a nation.

Ancient Life Along the Nile

by Kathleen Cox

PEARSON

Scott
Foresman

Editorial Offices: Glenview, Illinois • Parsippany, New Jersey • New York, New York
Sales Offices: Needham, Massachusetts • Duluth, Georgia • Glenview, Illinois
Coppell, Texas • Ontario, California • Mesa, Arizona

The Nile River

Thousands of years ago, groups of people who had once been wandering nomads built settlements along the northern end of Africa's Nile River. The Nile is the world's longest river. It flows from the mountains of central Africa north to the Mediterranean Sea. These settlers lived along a six-hundred-mile stretch of land that extended to the Mediterranean coast. Here, the year-round climate was generally mild and dry. Over time, the settlements joined together and formed a series of kingdoms that became the great ancient Egyptian civilization. These kingdoms founded many large cities such as Memphis and Thebes.

Rulers called pharaohs **reigned** over the people of ancient Egypt. The pharaohs owned all the land. They first called themselves servants of the Egyptian gods. Later, they began to think of themselves as gods who lived among the common people. Their subjects accepted this belief and honored the pharaohs, just as they honored the other gods and goddesses in the temples.

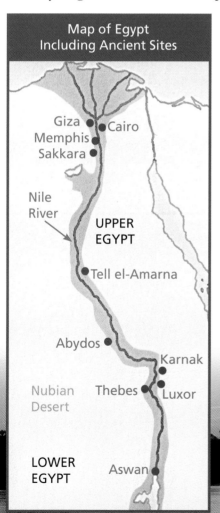

Map of Egypt Including Ancient Sites

Giza
Cairo
Memphis
Sakkara

Nile River

UPPER EGYPT

Tell el-Amarna

Abydos

Karnak

Nubian Desert

Thebes
Luxor

LOWER EGYPT

Aswan

Many cities grew up along the Nile River.

The ancient Egyptians believed that **immortal** gods and goddesses controlled everything that happened in their universe. The gods had power over the movement of the sun, the growth of the people's crops, the success of their hunting and fishing, and the flow of the Nile. The people worshipped their gods and goddesses and hoped that they, in return, would shower the people with good fortune.

Everyone in the kingdom of Egypt worked for the pharaoh. Priests watched over the spiritual well-being of the kingdom. Scribes, who were writers, kept records for the kingdom. They wrote the pharaoh's **decrees,** which informed the citizens of new laws and new taxes. Artists, sculptors, and architects created magnificent structures and artwork, which brought glory to the pharaohs. Other craftsmen shaped soft clay into useful storage containers and pots. Laborers created simple clay homes for the people, boats with delicate papyrus sails, and vast systems of canals that stretched throughout the land.

The Nile River was the center of life in ancient Egypt. Most people in Egypt were farmers. They depended on the river to water the crops that provided most of the harvested food for the kingdom. Other people raised livestock near the Nile. Fishermen brought in the daily catch from the river.

The temple of Ramses II sits on the banks of the Nile River, the center of ancient Egyptian culture.

Another group of citizens provided important services for the people, especially the upper class. Cobblers created leather sandals. Seamstresses and tailors stitched up comfortable clothing to wear in Egypt's warm climate. Jewelers made elaborate adornments out of bronze, gold, and colorful stones. Cooks created meals for the upper classes.

The workers who performed services in the kingdom still depended on the Nile, though not directly. Ancient Egypt did not have money as we know it today. People bartered, or traded, for goods. Cobblers bartered sandals for food. Farmers bartered bags of grain for pottery.

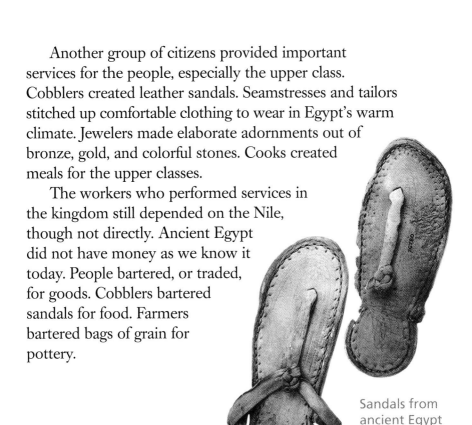

Sandals from ancient Egypt

Writing in Ancient Egypt

Only a very small number of men and women in ancient Egypt knew how to read and write. These people were called scribes. Some scribes were temple priests or administrators who ran the day-to-day activities of the kingdom. Others became architects who helped design the great structures and cities. Scribes worked under the pharaoh and other members of the royalty. They belonged to a very high class.

Scribes were a powerful group of people who could write the hieroglyphic language of Egypt.

In ancient Egypt, reading and writing meant learning how to read and draw a series of specific pictures. Each picture conveyed an idea or a sound. These picture words are called hieroglyphics. Hieroglyphic writing is one of the oldest systems of writing in the world.

Scribes had to memorize and master the creation of more than seven hundred hieroglyphics. Each picture had to be drawn exactly, or it could be misread. Scribes also studied mathematics and other subjects that were important to the pharaoh and the kingdom.

When scribes wrote hieroglyphic messages, they drew a group of pictures that told a story or conveyed important information. Much of the knowledge we have about daily life in ancient Egypt was actually gathered from hieroglyphics. They have been discovered on the walls of ancient buildings, on tablets, and on **artifacts** such as bits of pottery. Once archaeologists were able to read hieroglyphics, they could solve some of the mysteries of this ancient civilization.

The Nile River provided the tools that scribes used to write their everyday messages as well as the messages that would last for thousands of years. Tablets made from river mud were first used to record hieroglyphics. Later, they used papyrus, a paper-like material made from the papyrus plant. This plant was **abundant** on the banks of the Nile.

To make this paper, the papyrus plant was harvested by laborers. They cut down the stalks, which can grow to be ten feet long, and sliced them into thin strips. Then they soaked the stalks in water for a few days.

Once the water had softened the papyrus stalks, the laborers placed the strips on the ground and pounded them until most of the water drained away. The workers then arranged the strips into large sheets and placed them under boulders. The heavy weight caused the papyrus strips to bond together as they slowly dried out.

Since most people could not read, scribes acted as messengers as well. They would read a royal decree aloud so that citizens could learn about new laws and other decisions made by their pharaoh. This was one important way in which the pharaoh communicated with his subjects and kept them informed.

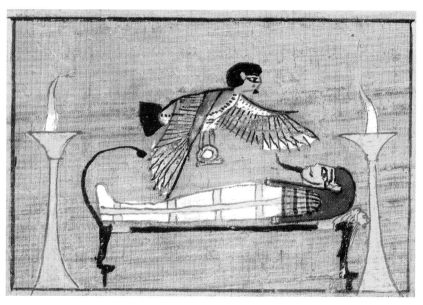

Papyrus was used for writing and for creating images like this one of a mummy and a spirit.

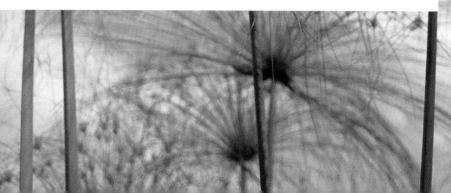

The Nile River was considered the source of life for the ancient Egyptians.

Ancient Egyptian Beliefs

Life for the Egyptians focused on the Nile River, which they believed was at the geographic center of the Earth. They believed that the Earth was flat. They had no way to know otherwise. They didn't have rugged ships that could sail through the rough waves of the oceans, where explorers might discover distant lands that existed beyond their horizon.

The Egyptian people thought that the Earth had started out as mud. They believed that their gods pushed up a mound of solid land called Egypt. The people of Egypt honored their gods for creating their land and the Nile.

Priests and priestesses were responsible for honoring and caring for the gods.

Egyptian priests and priestesses were responsible for making sure that the gods and goddesses were happy. These people were very powerful. If a pharaoh selected a man to become a priest or a woman to become a priestess, then the position would be passed on within the family from generation to generation. A father or mother would pass on the title to a son or daughter. From a young age, the chosen child served under his or her parent and learned the proper rituals and behavior.

All priests followed a strict code of conduct. They kept their bodies clean and pure by taking baths each day in sacred pools. They shaved their heads. They didn't want any of the filth of Earth to pollute their skin or their minds. After all, they were responsible for watching over the spiritual health of the people.

The priests and priestesses organized festivals, took care of the temples, and performed the rituals that marked each important stage of life. The people expected the priests and priestesses to be honorable and to please the gods and goddesses.

To hold their festivals and rituals, the ancient Egyptians built large temples along the Nile. The royal architects designed and supervised the creation of large building projects. Architects also designed the pyramids, which were enormous stone and clay tombs that honored each pharaoh and his family.

Archaeologists believe that the laborers, working under the hot sun for many years, slowly pushed gigantic stones up dirt ramps that were constructed along the walls of the pyramid, until they worked the last stone into place at the top.

The pyramids were so large that it took years to complete just one. The Great Pyramid at Giza is almost five hundred feet tall and covers nearly thirteen acres of land.

Architects and craftsmen also built the Great Sphinx. It was created out of a natural rock formation. Sculptors chiseled the sandstone and slowly shaped it into the head of a pharaoh. Archaeologists are still not sure which pharaoh the Great Sphinx is supposed to represent. The figure wears an ornate headdress and has the body of a lion.

The Great Sphinx is just one of many large structures built by the ancient Egyptians.

Anubis, the god of the dead (at left), stands by at a funeral.

The importance of the Nile carried over into the ancient Egyptian beliefs about the afterlife as well. The Egyptians believed that they should bury their dead on the western side of the great river. The sun set in the west, and they compared the setting sun, which brought an end to the day, to the end of life in this world.

For them, death was a transition. It was a temporary time that signified the end of life in this world and the beginning of life in another world. Because of their belief in an afterlife, the Egyptians took excellent care of their dead. If the dead were mistreated, the Egyptians believed that the spirits of the departed would make life miserable for the relatives who were still alive.

At someone's death, priests took the body and prepared it for its next life. The Egyptians believed that the spirit had already begun its journey to the next world. A priest had to preserve the body. That way, when the body followed the spirit, it would recognize the body and the two would be reunited.

Priests cleaned the body and carefully prepared it for burial. It took forty days to prepare the body. It was then wrapped with strips of linen. Inside the linen wrapping, priests placed amulets and other small treasures to protect the dead person on his or her journey to the afterlife.

The priests covered every inch of the skin with layers of linen to turn the deceased person into a mummy. Then they placed the mummy inside a coffin, which was often carved to look like the deceased.

The family presented the priests with some clothing, food, and other objects that they believed their relative needed for the journey. They wanted the deceased to live well in the hereafter. Some Egyptians asked the priests to include a miniature papyrus boat among the possessions. They believed that their relative would use the small boat to sail on the Nile River to the underworld, where this person would stay for **eternity.**

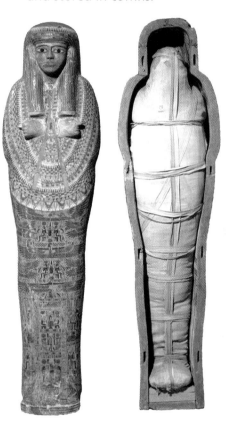

Bodies of the dead were wrapped in linen and stored in coffins.

A funeral barge transported the dead to the afterlife.

The Nile Floods

The Egyptians worshipped the god of the Nile River, Hapi. The river also had a strong influence on their economy. They thought of the river as their refuge from the desert that stretched in every direction. The ancient Egyptian civilization prospered because the Egyptians learned how to live in harmony with the powerful river, which cut through the center of their land.

Egypt receives very little rainfall, so the river water was extremely valuable. But the Nile River was a complicated neighbor. For much of the year it flowed calmly along its northerly course. But after the end of the summer harvest, heavy rains normally fell to the south of the Egyptian kingdom.

The rain-swollen Nile began to rush along its course through the land of ancient Egypt. Eventually, the water spilled over the banks of the river. Floodwaters rushed into the lowlands and covered everything in their path. Because of this seasonal flood, which the Egyptians called the Inundation, the people knew that they needed to build their homes on the highest land in their kingdom. The high elevation usually protected them from the destruction of the late summer flood.

The Egyptians welcomed the Inundation. The floodwaters deposited rich silt from the river onto the dry land. Once the waters **receded,** the silt was exposed and could be used for farming. At other times during the year, farmers had to build canals to get water from the river to their crops.

But sometimes the summer weather and the river didn't cooperate. At times too little summer rain fell to the south. The Nile failed to flow over its banks and saturate the surrounding land. It was difficult to irrigate the newly planted crops. The land dried out and the crops failed.

Sometimes there was too much rain in the summer, and the floodwaters caused terrible destruction. Raging waters washed away homes that were made of hardened clay. The structures simply crumbled and disappeared. Valuable orchards, which took years to establish in the soil, toppled over like flimsy matchsticks.

This picture, taken in the late 1800s, shows the seasonal flooding of the Nile River.

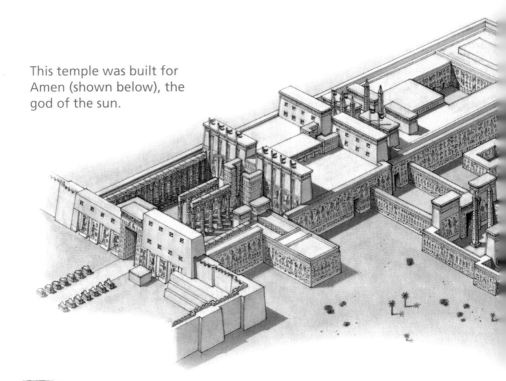

This temple was built for Amen (shown below), the god of the sun.

But when the flood followed its usual pattern, the people of Egypt benefited. They took time to thank their gods and goddesses for their good fortune. During the summer flood, the Egyptians held festivals to honor their gods.

One important festival was the festival of Opet. It honored Amen, the primary sun god, as well as Opet, Mut, and Khons. The festival went on for many days. This was an ideal time for a celebration since people could do very little work. The waters from the Nile River had filled their fields.

People flocked to the city of Karnak to attend the festival, which focused on a colorful procession. Priests removed the statues of the sacred gods from their temples, which were off-limits to common people. The priests put them inside a small shrine and placed the shrine on a small boat attached to poles.

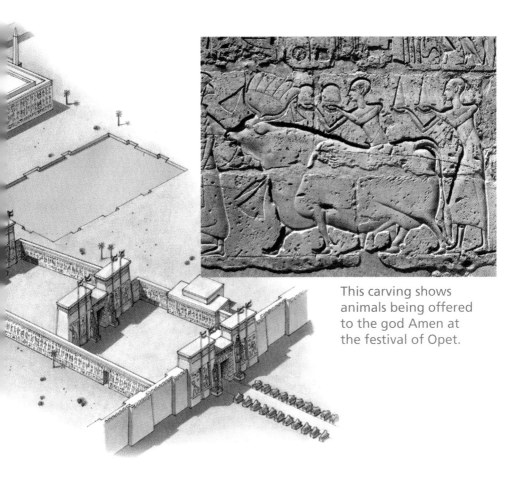

This carving shows animals being offered to the god Amen at the festival of Opet.

The priests balanced the poles on their shoulders. They slowly made their way through narrow streets to a second temple more than a mile away. The people followed close behind. Acrobats thrilled the people with their stunts. Musicians and singers played and sang along the way. The shrine was held high in the air for everyone to see.

When the priests reached the doors that led into the second temple, the pharaoh greeted the sacred statues. People danced. Drums rolled. The priests and the pharaoh took the small shrine with its statues inside the temple, where the pharaoh received divine blessings from the god Amen. Sometimes this entire journey and festival procession took place on boats that floated on the Nile between these two temples.

Farming Along the Nile

When the floodwaters receded from the lowlands, they replenished the farmland by leaving behind a rich coat of silt, or topsoil. This black soil was filled with nutrients such as nitrogen, which enriched the soil. The receding waters signaled the start of the annual season of rebirth and renewal. This was the time for farmers to go into their fields and plant their crops for the next year.

Planting conditions after the flood were perfect. The sun shone brightly, which was necessary for the growth of healthy, strong plants. Many inches of the soil, including the fertile top layer, were extremely muddy from the flood.

The mud made it easier for the farmers to plant their seeds. They didn't have to work a hoe through hard land or struggle to turn over their soil. They didn't have to water their fields once they planted their seeds. The flood did these chores for the farmers.

The farmers grew a wide variety of crops. They planted grains such as barley and wheat. They planted vegetables such as beans, chickpeas, cucumbers, lettuce, and onions. On higher land, the Egyptians created vineyards and orchards. The trees bore fruits such as pomegranates, figs, and dates. The farmers planted gardens of herbs and spices such as dill, thyme, sage, and cumin to flavor their food.

Many ancient Egyptians were farmers or herders.

Many animals were drawn to the Nile River, where they took refuge under the shade of palm trees and drank from the river. Ducks and geese waddled along the riverbanks or swam in the water. Fish, crocodiles, and hippopotamuses also made the river their home. All these creatures were hunted by the Egyptians.

Only the upper class and royalty could afford meals that included meat. The lower classes usually ate vegetarian meals, which they enjoyed with homemade bread. They spiced up their dishes with dill and cumin or sweetened them with honey. They also ate watermelon, grapes, figs, and dates.

The floodwaters also helped the Egyptians devise irrigation systems, which were important along the Nile River. The crops and orchards received plenty of sunlight, but they also needed a lot of water to produce an abundant harvest. The people needed water for drinking and bathing.

The Egyptians took advantage of natural **levees** created by rocks, dead trees, and debris from abandoned settlements. These objects were tossed into piles by the raging floodwaters. Once the water showed signs of receding, laborers ventured into the mud and propped up the piles to create sidewalls. They built the walls into networks of ditches and simple canals that trapped the water. Farmers used the trapped water to irrigate their crops. Other people used the water for their needs during the drier months.

The farmers also built their own canals to irrigate crops. These were especially important for their orchards and smaller gardens. As time went on, the irrigation systems became more complicated. The ancient Egyptians did their best to keep water flowing to their fields. Their hard work created large harvests that made Egypt a very rich kingdom.

These are the flowers of flax plants.

Many farmers and their families grew flax, which was used to produce linen. Linen was used to make clothing. This important plant was harvested while it was still blooming. Children piled the plants high on their heads. Adults with big bundles stacked in their arms carried the valuable plants from the fields to a flat area where the flax could dry out in the sun. Then women spun the fibers of the flax into thread that was woven into linen.

Ancient flax cord

Clothing was simple and made of linen.

Egyptian Fashion

Clothing in ancient Egypt was relatively simple and functional. Upper-class men usually wore short white skirts, or kilts. Older men wore long comfortable robes that swept down to their ankles.

Upper-class women dressed in close-fitting robes. Sometimes they added a cape-style cloak over their shoulders in the evenings, or if there was a rare cool breeze. The women's hair, jewelry, and elaborate makeup, which was especially dramatic around their eyes, held everyone's attention, not their clothing.

Lower-class men and women wore kilts made of a rougher linen. They were usually midcalf length. This simple attire provided comfort and ease of movement when they worked in the heat or in the fields. Children also wore very simple kilts as they worked beside their parents.

Both sexes cared deeply about their appearance, especially members of the upper class. After they bathed, they dabbed on fragrant oils and creams to protect their skin from the dry heat.

Wealthy men and women spent a good deal of time grooming their hair. They rubbed it with wax from beehives, which held the style and made the hair shine. Many wealthy men and women, including the pharaohs, wore dark wigs designed in elaborate hairstyles.

The people of ancient Egypt loved jewelry. Men and women wore stone-studded metal collars and necklaces that draped down their necks. They wore wide cuffs of bronze, gold, and precious stones around their upper arms, wrists, and ankles. Their fingers sparkled with rings. So did their toes, which would peek out of their leather sandals.

For many centuries the Egyptians retained their customs, from their style of clothing to their religious beliefs. Their kingdom flourished along the Nile River. And for a long time, their civilization prospered.

Egyptians used combs and other objects to be fashionable.

Glossary

abundant *adj.* more than enough; very plentiful.

artifacts *n.* any items made by human skill or work, especially tools or weapons.

decrees *n.* decisions ordered by authority; laws.

eternity *n.* all time; an endless time period.

immortal *adj.* living forever, never dying, everlasting.

levees *n.* high banks built to keep a river from overflowing.

receded *v.* moved backward, withdrew.

reigned *v.* ruled over, as a monarch rules over a nation.

Ancient Life Along the Nile

by Kathleen Cox

PEARSON

Scott Foresman

Editorial Offices: Glenview, Illinois • Parsippany, New Jersey • New York, New York
Sales Offices: Needham, Massachusetts • Duluth, Georgia • Glenview, Illinois
Coppell, Texas • Ontario, California • Mesa, Arizona

The Nile River

Thousands of years ago, groups of people who had once been wandering nomads built settlements along the northern end of Africa's Nile River. The Nile is the world's longest river. It flows from the mountains of central Africa north to the Mediterranean Sea. These settlers lived along a six-hundred-mile stretch of land that extended to the Mediterranean coast. Here, the year-round climate was generally mild and dry. Over time, the settlements joined together and formed a series of kingdoms that became the great ancient Egyptian civilization. These kingdoms founded many large cities such as Memphis and Thebes.

Rulers called pharaohs **reigned** over the people of ancient Egypt. The pharaohs owned all the land. They first called themselves servants of the Egyptian gods. Later, they began to think of themselves as gods who lived among the common people. Their subjects accepted this belief and honored the pharaohs, just as they honored the other gods and goddesses in the temples.

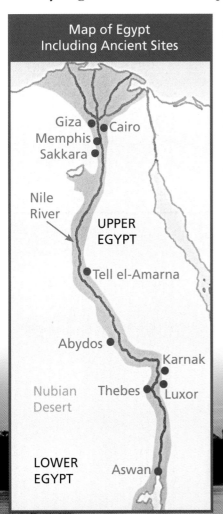

Map of Egypt Including Ancient Sites

Giza
Cairo
Memphis
Sakkara

Nile River

UPPER EGYPT

Tell el-Amarna

Abydos

Karnak

Nubian Desert

Thebes
Luxor

LOWER EGYPT

Aswan

Many cities grew up along the Nile River.

The ancient Egyptians believed that **immortal** gods and goddesses controlled everything that happened in their universe. The gods had power over the movement of the sun, the growth of the people's crops, the success of their hunting and fishing, and the flow of the Nile. The people worshipped their gods and goddesses and hoped that they, in return, would shower the people with good fortune.

Everyone in the kingdom of Egypt worked for the pharaoh. Priests watched over the spiritual well-being of the kingdom. Scribes, who were writers, kept records for the kingdom. They wrote the pharaoh's **decrees,** which informed the citizens of new laws and new taxes. Artists, sculptors, and architects created magnificent structures and artwork, which brought glory to the pharaohs. Other craftsmen shaped soft clay into useful storage containers and pots. Laborers created simple clay homes for the people, boats with delicate papyrus sails, and vast systems of canals that stretched throughout the land.

The Nile River was the center of life in ancient Egypt. Most people in Egypt were farmers. They depended on the river to water the crops that provided most of the harvested food for the kingdom. Other people raised livestock near the Nile. Fishermen brought in the daily catch from the river.

The temple of Ramses II sits on the banks of the Nile River, the center of ancient Egyptian culture.

Another group of citizens provided important services for the people, especially the upper class. Cobblers created leather sandals. Seamstresses and tailors stitched up comfortable clothing to wear in Egypt's warm climate. Jewelers made elaborate adornments out of bronze, gold, and colorful stones. Cooks created meals for the upper classes.

The workers who performed services in the kingdom still depended on the Nile, though not directly. Ancient Egypt did not have money as we know it today. People bartered, or traded, for goods. Cobblers bartered sandals for food. Farmers bartered bags of grain for pottery.

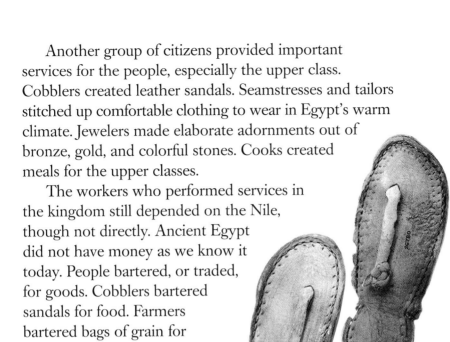

Sandals from ancient Egypt

Writing in Ancient Egypt

Only a very small number of men and women in ancient Egypt knew how to read and write. These people were called scribes. Some scribes were temple priests or administrators who ran the day-to-day activities of the kingdom. Others became architects who helped design the great structures and cities. Scribes worked under the pharaoh and other members of the royalty. They belonged to a very high class.

Scribes were a powerful group of people who could write the hieroglyphic language of Egypt.

In ancient Egypt, reading and writing meant learning how to read and draw a series of specific pictures. Each picture conveyed an idea or a sound. These picture words are called hieroglyphics. Hieroglyphic writing is one of the oldest systems of writing in the world.

Scribes had to memorize and master the creation of more than seven hundred hieroglyphics. Each picture had to be drawn exactly, or it could be misread. Scribes also studied mathematics and other subjects that were important to the pharaoh and the kingdom.

When scribes wrote hieroglyphic messages, they drew a group of pictures that told a story or conveyed important information. Much of the knowledge we have about daily life in ancient Egypt was actually gathered from hieroglyphics. They have been discovered on the walls of ancient buildings, on tablets, and on **artifacts** such as bits of pottery. Once archaeologists were able to read hieroglyphics, they could solve some of the mysteries of this ancient civilization.

The Nile River provided the tools that scribes used to write their everyday messages as well as the messages that would last for thousands of years. Tablets made from river mud were first used to record hieroglyphics. Later, they used papyrus, a paper-like material made from the papyrus plant. This plant was **abundant** on the banks of the Nile.

To make this paper, the papyrus plant was harvested by laborers. They cut down the stalks, which can grow to be ten feet long, and sliced them into thin strips. Then they soaked the stalks in water for a few days.

Once the water had softened the papyrus stalks, the laborers placed the strips on the ground and pounded them until most of the water drained away. The workers then arranged the strips into large sheets and placed them under boulders. The heavy weight caused the papyrus strips to bond together as they slowly dried out.

Since most people could not read, scribes acted as messengers as well. They would read a royal decree aloud so that citizens could learn about new laws and other decisions made by their pharaoh. This was one important way in which the pharaoh communicated with his subjects and kept them informed.

Papyrus was used for writing and for creating images like this one of a mummy and a spirit.

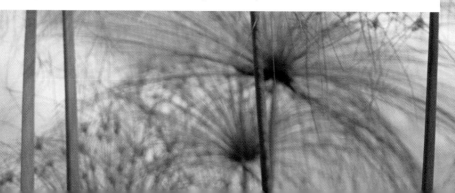

The Nile River was considered the source of life for the ancient Egyptians.

Ancient Egyptian Beliefs

Life for the Egyptians focused on the Nile River, which they believed was at the geographic center of the Earth. They believed that the Earth was flat. They had no way to know otherwise. They didn't have rugged ships that could sail through the rough waves of the oceans, where explorers might discover distant lands that existed beyond their horizon.

The Egyptian people thought that the Earth had started out as mud. They believed that their gods pushed up a mound of solid land called Egypt. The people of Egypt honored their gods for creating their land and the Nile.

Priests and priestesses were responsible for honoring and caring for the gods.

Egyptian priests and priestesses were responsible for making sure that the gods and goddesses were happy. These people were very powerful. If a pharaoh selected a man to become a priest or a woman to become a priestess, then the position would be passed on within the family from generation to generation. A father or mother would pass on the title to a son or daughter. From a young age, the chosen child served under his or her parent and learned the proper rituals and behavior.

All priests followed a strict code of conduct. They kept their bodies clean and pure by taking baths each day in sacred pools. They shaved their heads. They didn't want any of the filth of Earth to pollute their skin or their minds. After all, they were responsible for watching over the spiritual health of the people.

The priests and priestesses organized festivals, took care of the temples, and performed the rituals that marked each important stage of life. The people expected the priests and priestesses to be honorable and to please the gods and goddesses.

To hold their festivals and rituals, the ancient Egyptians built large temples along the Nile. The royal architects designed and supervised the creation of large building projects. Architects also designed the pyramids, which were enormous stone and clay tombs that honored each pharaoh and his family.

Archaeologists believe that the laborers, working under the hot sun for many years, slowly pushed gigantic stones up dirt ramps that were constructed along the walls of the pyramid, until they worked the last stone into place at the top.

The pyramids were so large that it took years to complete just one. The Great Pyramid at Giza is almost five hundred feet tall and covers nearly thirteen acres of land.

Architects and craftsmen also built the Great Sphinx. It was created out of a natural rock formation. Sculptors chiseled the sandstone and slowly shaped it into the head of a pharaoh. Archaeologists are still not sure which pharaoh the Great Sphinx is supposed to represent. The figure wears an ornate headdress and has the body of a lion.

The Great Sphinx is just one of many large structures built by the ancient Egyptians.

Anubis, the god of the dead (at left), stands by at a funeral.

The importance of the Nile carried over into the ancient Egyptian beliefs about the afterlife as well. The Egyptians believed that they should bury their dead on the western side of the great river. The sun set in the west, and they compared the setting sun, which brought an end to the day, to the end of life in this world.

For them, death was a transition. It was a temporary time that signified the end of life in this world and the beginning of life in another world. Because of their belief in an afterlife, the Egyptians took excellent care of their dead. If the dead were mistreated, the Egyptians believed that the spirits of the departed would make life miserable for the relatives who were still alive.

At someone's death, priests took the body and prepared it for its next life. The Egyptians believed that the spirit had already begun its journey to the next world. A priest had to preserve the body. That way, when the body followed the spirit, it would recognize the body and the two would be reunited.

Priests cleaned the body and carefully prepared it for burial. It took forty days to prepare the body. It was then wrapped with strips of linen. Inside the linen wrapping, priests placed amulets and other small treasures to protect the dead person on his or her journey to the afterlife.

The priests covered every inch of the skin with layers of linen to turn the deceased person into a mummy. Then they placed the mummy inside a coffin, which was often carved to look like the deceased.

The family presented the priests with some clothing, food, and other objects that they believed their relative needed for the journey. They wanted the deceased to live well in the hereafter. Some Egyptians asked the priests to include a miniature papyrus boat among the possessions. They believed that their relative would use the small boat to sail on the Nile River to the underworld, where this person would stay for **eternity.**

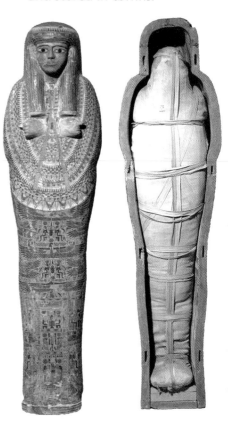

Bodies of the dead were wrapped in linen and stored in coffins.

A funeral barge transported the dead to the afterlife.

The Nile Floods

The Egyptians worshipped the god of the Nile River, Hapi. The river also had a strong influence on their economy. They thought of the river as their refuge from the desert that stretched in every direction. The ancient Egyptian civilization prospered because the Egyptians learned how to live in harmony with the powerful river, which cut through the center of their land.

Egypt receives very little rainfall, so the river water was extremely valuable. But the Nile River was a complicated neighbor. For much of the year it flowed calmly along its northerly course. But after the end of the summer harvest, heavy rains normally fell to the south of the Egyptian kingdom.

The rain-swollen Nile began to rush along its course through the land of ancient Egypt. Eventually, the water spilled over the banks of the river. Floodwaters rushed into the lowlands and covered everything in their path. Because of this seasonal flood, which the Egyptians called the Inundation, the people knew that they needed to build their homes on the highest land in their kingdom. The high elevation usually protected them from the destruction of the late summer flood.

The Egyptians welcomed the Inundation. The floodwaters deposited rich silt from the river onto the dry land. Once the waters **receded,** the silt was exposed and could be used for farming. At other times during the year, farmers had to build canals to get water from the river to their crops.

But sometimes the summer weather and the river didn't cooperate. At times too little summer rain fell to the south. The Nile failed to flow over its banks and saturate the surrounding land. It was difficult to irrigate the newly planted crops. The land dried out and the crops failed.

Sometimes there was too much rain in the summer, and the floodwaters caused terrible destruction. Raging waters washed away homes that were made of hardened clay. The structures simply crumbled and disappeared. Valuable orchards, which took years to establish in the soil, toppled over like flimsy matchsticks.

This picture, taken in the late 1800s, shows the seasonal flooding of the Nile River.

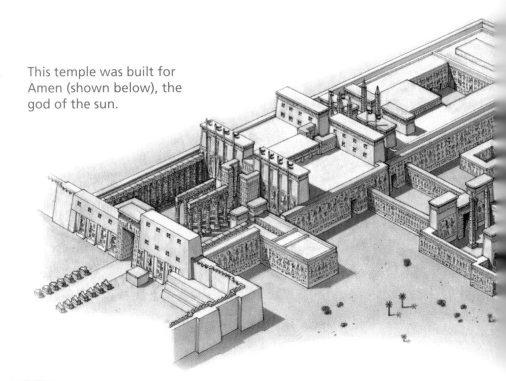

This temple was built for Amen (shown below), the god of the sun.

But when the flood followed its usual pattern, the people of Egypt benefited. They took time to thank their gods and goddesses for their good fortune. During the summer flood, the Egyptians held festivals to honor their gods.

One important festival was the festival of Opet. It honored Amen, the primary sun god, as well as Opet, Mut, and Khons. The festival went on for many days. This was an ideal time for a celebration since people could do very little work. The waters from the Nile River had filled their fields.

People flocked to the city of Karnak to attend the festival, which focused on a colorful procession. Priests removed the statues of the sacred gods from their temples, which were off-limits to common people. The priests put them inside a small shrine and placed the shrine on a small boat attached to poles.

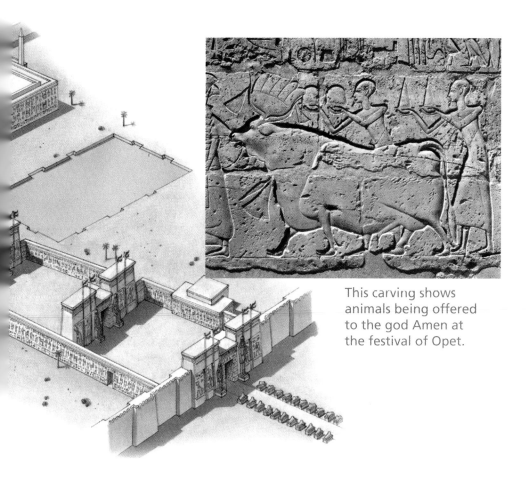

This carving shows animals being offered to the god Amen at the festival of Opet.

The priests balanced the poles on their shoulders. They slowly made their way through narrow streets to a second temple more than a mile away. The people followed close behind. Acrobats thrilled the people with their stunts. Musicians and singers played and sang along the way. The shrine was held high in the air for everyone to see.

When the priests reached the doors that led into the second temple, the pharaoh greeted the sacred statues. People danced. Drums rolled. The priests and the pharaoh took the small shrine with its statues inside the temple, where the pharaoh received divine blessings from the god Amen. Sometimes this entire journey and festival procession took place on boats that floated on the Nile between these two temples.

Farming Along the Nile

When the floodwaters receded from the lowlands, they replenished the farmland by leaving behind a rich coat of silt, or topsoil. This black soil was filled with nutrients such as nitrogen, which enriched the soil. The receding waters signaled the start of the annual season of rebirth and renewal. This was the time for farmers to go into their fields and plant their crops for the next year.

Planting conditions after the flood were perfect. The sun shone brightly, which was necessary for the growth of healthy, strong plants. Many inches of the soil, including the fertile top layer, were extremely muddy from the flood.

The mud made it easier for the farmers to plant their seeds. They didn't have to work a hoe through hard land or struggle to turn over their soil. They didn't have to water their fields once they planted their seeds. The flood did these chores for the farmers.

The farmers grew a wide variety of crops. They planted grains such as barley and wheat. They planted vegetables such as beans, chickpeas, cucumbers, lettuce, and onions. On higher land, the Egyptians created vineyards and orchards. The trees bore fruits such as pomegranates, figs, and dates. The farmers planted gardens of herbs and spices such as dill, thyme, sage, and cumin to flavor their food.

Many ancient Egyptians were farmers or herders.

Many animals were drawn to the Nile River, where they took refuge under the shade of palm trees and drank from the river. Ducks and geese waddled along the riverbanks or swam in the water. Fish, crocodiles, and hippopotamuses also made the river their home. All these creatures were hunted by the Egyptians.

Only the upper class and royalty could afford meals that included meat. The lower classes usually ate vegetarian meals, which they enjoyed with homemade bread. They spiced up their dishes with dill and cumin or sweetened them with honey. They also ate watermelon, grapes, figs, and dates.

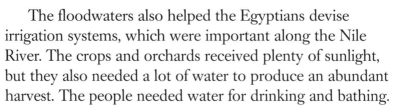

The floodwaters also helped the Egyptians devise irrigation systems, which were important along the Nile River. The crops and orchards received plenty of sunlight, but they also needed a lot of water to produce an abundant harvest. The people needed water for drinking and bathing.

The Egyptians took advantage of natural **levees** created by rocks, dead trees, and debris from abandoned settlements. These objects were tossed into piles by the raging floodwaters. Once the water showed signs of receding, laborers ventured into the mud and propped up the piles to create sidewalls. They built the walls into networks of ditches and simple canals that trapped the water. Farmers used the trapped water to irrigate their crops. Other people used the water for their needs during the drier months.

The farmers also built their own canals to irrigate crops. These were especially important for their orchards and smaller gardens. As time went on, the irrigation systems became more complicated. The ancient Egyptians did their best to keep water flowing to their fields. Their hard work created large harvests that made Egypt a very rich kingdom.

These are the flowers of flax plants.

Many farmers and their families grew flax, which was used to produce linen. Linen was used to make clothing. This important plant was harvested while it was still blooming. Children piled the plants high on their heads. Adults with big bundles stacked in their arms carried the valuable plants from the fields to a flat area where the flax could dry out in the sun. Then women spun the fibers of the flax into thread that was woven into linen.

Ancient flax cord

Clothing was simple
and made of linen.

Egyptian Fashion

Clothing in ancient Egypt was relatively simple and
functional. Upper-class men usually wore short white skirts,
or kilts. Older men wore long comfortable robes that swept
down to their ankles.

Upper-class women dressed in close-fitting robes.
Sometimes they added a cape-style cloak over their
shoulders in the evenings, or if there was a rare cool breeze.
The women's hair, jewelry, and elaborate makeup, which
was especially dramatic around their eyes, held everyone's
attention, not their clothing.

Lower-class men and women wore kilts made of a
rougher linen. They were usually midcalf length. This
simple attire provided comfort and ease of movement when
they worked in the heat or in the fields. Children also wore
very simple kilts as they worked beside their parents.

Both sexes cared deeply about their appearance, especially members of the upper class. After they bathed, they dabbed on fragrant oils and creams to protect their skin from the dry heat.

Wealthy men and women spent a good deal of time grooming their hair. They rubbed it with wax from beehives, which held the style and made the hair shine. Many wealthy men and women, including the pharaohs, wore dark wigs designed in elaborate hairstyles.

The people of ancient Egypt loved jewelry. Men and women wore stone-studded metal collars and necklaces that draped down their necks. They wore wide cuffs of bronze, gold, and precious stones around their upper arms, wrists, and ankles. Their fingers sparkled with rings. So did their toes, which would peek out of their leather sandals.

For many centuries the Egyptians retained their customs, from their style of clothing to their religious beliefs. Their kingdom flourished along the Nile River. And for a long time, their civilization prospered.

Egyptians used combs and other objects to be fashionable.

Glossary

abundant *adj.* more than enough; very plentiful.

artifacts *n.* any items made by human skill or work, especially tools or weapons.

decrees *n.* decisions ordered by authority; laws.

eternity *n.* all time; an endless time period.

immortal *adj.* living forever, never dying, everlasting.

levees *n.* high banks built to keep a river from overflowing.

receded *v.* moved backward, withdrew.

reigned *v.* ruled over, as a monarch rules over a nation.

Ancient Life Along the Nile

by Kathleen Cox

Editorial Offices: Glenview, Illinois • Parsippany, New Jersey • New York, New York
Sales Offices: Needham, Massachusetts • Duluth, Georgia • Glenview, Illinois
Coppell, Texas • Ontario, California • Mesa, Arizona

ISBN: 0-328-13620-4

3 4 5 6 7 8 9 10 V0G1 14 13 12 11 10 09 08 07 06

The Nile River

Thousands of years ago, groups of people who had once been wandering nomads built settlements along the northern end of Africa's Nile River. The Nile is the world's longest river. It flows from the mountains of central Africa north to the Mediterranean Sea. These settlers lived along a six-hundred-mile stretch of land that extended to the Mediterranean coast. Here, the year-round climate was generally mild and dry. Over time, the settlements joined together and formed a series of kingdoms that became the great ancient Egyptian civilization. These kingdoms founded many large cities such as Memphis and Thebes.

Rulers called pharaohs **reigned** over the people of ancient Egypt. The pharaohs owned all the land. They first called themselves servants of the Egyptian gods. Later, they began to think of themselves as gods who lived among the common people. Their subjects accepted this belief and honored the pharaohs, just as they honored the other gods and goddesses in the temples.

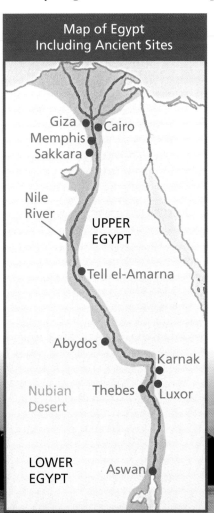

Map of Egypt
Including Ancient Sites

Giza • • Cairo
Memphis •
Sakkara •

Nile
River

UPPER
EGYPT

• Tell el-Amarna

Abydos •

Karnak •

Nubian   Thebes • • Luxor
Desert

LOWER
EGYPT   Aswan •

Many cities grew up along the Nile River.

The ancient Egyptians believed that **immortal** gods and goddesses controlled everything that happened in their universe. The gods had power over the movement of the sun, the growth of the people's crops, the success of their hunting and fishing, and the flow of the Nile. The people worshipped their gods and goddesses and hoped that they, in return, would shower the people with good fortune.

Everyone in the kingdom of Egypt worked for the pharaoh. Priests watched over the spiritual well-being of the kingdom. Scribes, who were writers, kept records for the kingdom. They wrote the pharaoh's **decrees,** which informed the citizens of new laws and new taxes. Artists, sculptors, and architects created magnificent structures and artwork, which brought glory to the pharaohs. Other craftsmen shaped soft clay into useful storage containers and pots. Laborers created simple clay homes for the people, boats with delicate papyrus sails, and vast systems of canals that stretched throughout the land.

The Nile River was the center of life in ancient Egypt. Most people in Egypt were farmers. They depended on the river to water the crops that provided most of the harvested food for the kingdom. Other people raised livestock near the Nile. Fishermen brought in the daily catch from the river.

The temple of Ramses II sits on the banks of the Nile River, the center of ancient Egyptian culture.

Another group of citizens provided important services for the people, especially the upper class. Cobblers created leather sandals. Seamstresses and tailors stitched up comfortable clothing to wear in Egypt's warm climate. Jewelers made elaborate adornments out of bronze, gold, and colorful stones. Cooks created meals for the upper classes.

The workers who performed services in the kingdom still depended on the Nile, though not directly. Ancient Egypt did not have money as we know it today. People bartered, or traded, for goods. Cobblers bartered sandals for food. Farmers bartered bags of grain for pottery.

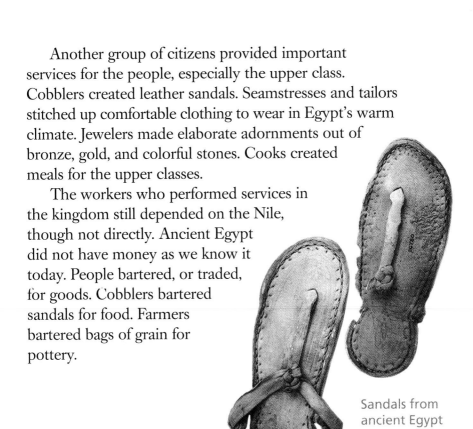

Sandals from ancient Egypt

Writing in Ancient Egypt

Only a very small number of men and women in ancient Egypt knew how to read and write. These people were called scribes. Some scribes were temple priests or administrators who ran the day-to-day activities of the kingdom. Others became architects who helped design the great structures and cities. Scribes worked under the pharaoh and other members of the royalty. They belonged to a very high class.

Scribes were a powerful group of people who could write the hieroglyphic language of Egypt.

In ancient Egypt, reading and writing meant learning how to read and draw a series of specific pictures. Each picture conveyed an idea or a sound. These picture words are called hieroglyphics. Hieroglyphic writing is one of the oldest systems of writing in the world.

Scribes had to memorize and master the creation of more than seven hundred hieroglyphics. Each picture had to be drawn exactly, or it could be misread. Scribes also studied mathematics and other subjects that were important to the pharaoh and the kingdom.

When scribes wrote hieroglyphic messages, they drew a group of pictures that told a story or conveyed important information. Much of the knowledge we have about daily life in ancient Egypt was actually gathered from hieroglyphics. They have been discovered on the walls of ancient buildings, on tablets, and on **artifacts** such as bits of pottery. Once archaeologists were able to read hieroglyphics, they could solve some of the mysteries of this ancient civilization.

The Nile River provided the tools that scribes used to write their everyday messages as well as the messages that would last for thousands of years. Tablets made from river mud were first used to record hieroglyphics. Later, they used papyrus, a paper-like material made from the papyrus plant. This plant was **abundant** on the banks of the Nile.

To make this paper, the papyrus plant was harvested by laborers. They cut down the stalks, which can grow to be ten feet long, and sliced them into thin strips. Then they soaked the stalks in water for a few days.

Once the water had softened the papyrus stalks, the laborers placed the strips on the ground and pounded them until most of the water drained away. The workers then arranged the strips into large sheets and placed them under boulders. The heavy weight caused the papyrus strips to bond together as they slowly dried out.

Since most people could not read, scribes acted as messengers as well. They would read a royal decree aloud so that citizens could learn about new laws and other decisions made by their pharaoh. This was one important way in which the pharaoh communicated with his subjects and kept them informed.

Papyrus was used for writing and for creating images like this one of a mummy and a spirit.

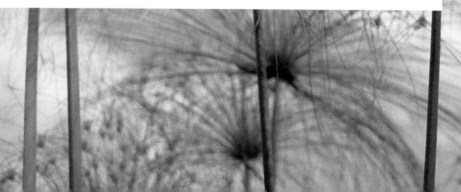

The Nile River was considered the source of life for the ancient Egyptians.

Ancient Egyptian Beliefs

Life for the Egyptians focused on the Nile River, which they believed was at the geographic center of the Earth. They believed that the Earth was flat. They had no way to know otherwise. They didn't have rugged ships that could sail through the rough waves of the oceans, where explorers might discover distant lands that existed beyond their horizon.

The Egyptian people thought that the Earth had started out as mud. They believed that their gods pushed up a mound of solid land called Egypt. The people of Egypt honored their gods for creating their land and the Nile.

Priests and priestesses were responsible for honoring and caring for the gods.

Egyptian priests and priestesses were responsible for making sure that the gods and goddesses were happy. These people were very powerful. If a pharaoh selected a man to become a priest or a woman to become a priestess, then the position would be passed on within the family from generation to generation. A father or mother would pass on the title to a son or daughter. From a young age, the chosen child served under his or her parent and learned the proper rituals and behavior.

All priests followed a strict code of conduct. They kept their bodies clean and pure by taking baths each day in sacred pools. They shaved their heads. They didn't want any of the filth of Earth to pollute their skin or their minds. After all, they were responsible for watching over the spiritual health of the people.

The priests and priestesses organized festivals, took care of the temples, and performed the rituals that marked each important stage of life. The people expected the priests and priestesses to be honorable and to please the gods and goddesses.

To hold their festivals and rituals, the ancient Egyptians built large temples along the Nile. The royal architects designed and supervised the creation of large building projects. Architects also designed the pyramids, which were enormous stone and clay tombs that honored each pharaoh and his family.

Archaeologists believe that the laborers, working under the hot sun for many years, slowly pushed gigantic stones up dirt ramps that were constructed along the walls of the pyramid, until they worked the last stone into place at the top.

The pyramids were so large that it took years to complete just one. The Great Pyramid at Giza is almost five hundred feet tall and covers nearly thirteen acres of land.

Architects and craftsmen also built the Great Sphinx. It was created out of a natural rock formation. Sculptors chiseled the sandstone and slowly shaped it into the head of a pharaoh. Archaeologists are still not sure which pharaoh the Great Sphinx is supposed to represent. The figure wears an ornate headdress and has the body of a lion.

The Great Sphinx is just one of many large structures built by the ancient Egyptians.

Anubis, the god of the dead (at left), stands by at a funeral.

The importance of the Nile carried over into the ancient Egyptian beliefs about the afterlife as well. The Egyptians believed that they should bury their dead on the western side of the great river. The sun set in the west, and they compared the setting sun, which brought an end to the day, to the end of life in this world.

For them, death was a transition. It was a temporary time that signified the end of life in this world and the beginning of life in another world. Because of their belief in an afterlife, the Egyptians took excellent care of their dead. If the dead were mistreated, the Egyptians believed that the spirits of the departed would make life miserable for the relatives who were still alive.

At someone's death, priests took the body and prepared it for its next life. The Egyptians believed that the spirit had already begun its journey to the next world. A priest had to preserve the body. That way, when the body followed the spirit, it would recognize the body and the two would be reunited.

Priests cleaned the body and carefully prepared it for burial. It took forty days to prepare the body. It was then wrapped with strips of linen. Inside the linen wrapping, priests placed amulets and other small treasures to protect the dead person on his or her journey to the afterlife.

The priests covered every inch of the skin with layers of linen to turn the deceased person into a mummy. Then they placed the mummy inside a coffin, which was often carved to look like the deceased.

The family presented the priests with some clothing, food, and other objects that they believed their relative needed for the journey. They wanted the deceased to live well in the hereafter. Some Egyptians asked the priests to include a miniature papyrus boat among the possessions. They believed that their relative would use the small boat to sail on the Nile River to the underworld, where this person would stay for **eternity.**

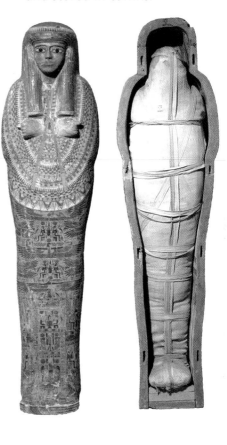

Bodies of the dead were wrapped in linen and stored in coffins.

A funeral barge transported the dead to the afterlife.

The Nile Floods

The Egyptians worshipped the god of the Nile River, Hapi. The river also had a strong influence on their economy. They thought of the river as their refuge from the desert that stretched in every direction. The ancient Egyptian civilization prospered because the Egyptians learned how to live in harmony with the powerful river, which cut through the center of their land.

Egypt receives very little rainfall, so the river water was extremely valuable. But the Nile River was a complicated neighbor. For much of the year it flowed calmly along its northerly course. But after the end of the summer harvest, heavy rains normally fell to the south of the Egyptian kingdom.

The rain-swollen Nile began to rush along its course through the land of ancient Egypt. Eventually, the water spilled over the banks of the river. Floodwaters rushed into the lowlands and covered everything in their path. Because of this seasonal flood, which the Egyptians called the Inundation, the people knew that they needed to build their homes on the highest land in their kingdom. The high elevation usually protected them from the destruction of the late summer flood.

The Egyptians welcomed the Inundation. The floodwaters deposited rich silt from the river onto the dry land. Once the waters **receded,** the silt was exposed and could be used for farming. At other times during the year, farmers had to build canals to get water from the river to their crops.

But sometimes the summer weather and the river didn't cooperate. At times too little summer rain fell to the south. The Nile failed to flow over its banks and saturate the surrounding land. It was difficult to irrigate the newly planted crops. The land dried out and the crops failed.

Sometimes there was too much rain in the summer, and the floodwaters caused terrible destruction. Raging waters washed away homes that were made of hardened clay. The structures simply crumbled and disappeared. Valuable orchards, which took years to establish in the soil, toppled over like flimsy matchsticks.

This picture, taken in the late 1800s, shows the seasonal flooding of the Nile River.

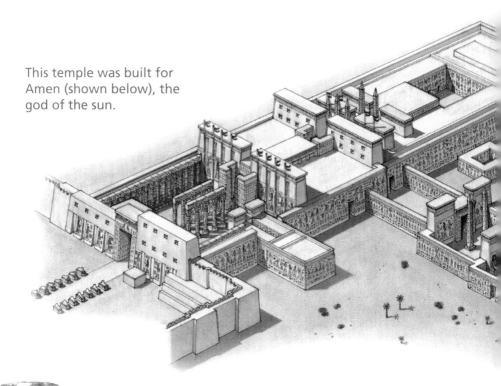

This temple was built for Amen (shown below), the god of the sun.

But when the flood followed its usual pattern, the people of Egypt benefited. They took time to thank their gods and goddesses for their good fortune. During the summer flood, the Egyptians held festivals to honor their gods.

One important festival was the festival of Opet. It honored Amen, the primary sun god, as well as Opet, Mut, and Khons. The festival went on for many days. This was an ideal time for a celebration since people could do very little work. The waters from the Nile River had filled their fields.

People flocked to the city of Karnak to attend the festival, which focused on a colorful procession. Priests removed the statues of the sacred gods from their temples, which were off-limits to common people. The priests put them inside a small shrine and placed the shrine on a small boat attached to poles.

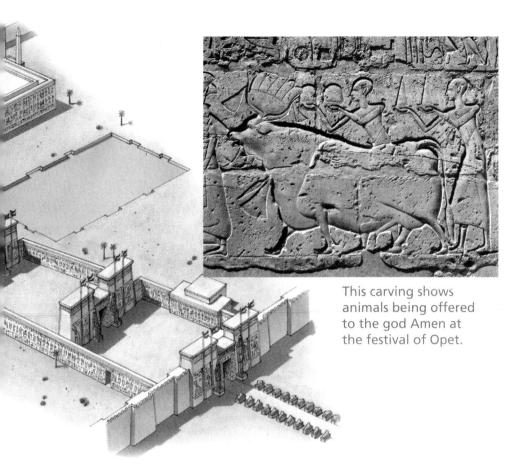

This carving shows animals being offered to the god Amen at the festival of Opet.

The priests balanced the poles on their shoulders. They slowly made their way through narrow streets to a second temple more than a mile away. The people followed close behind. Acrobats thrilled the people with their stunts. Musicians and singers played and sang along the way. The shrine was held high in the air for everyone to see.

When the priests reached the doors that led into the second temple, the pharaoh greeted the sacred statues. People danced. Drums rolled. The priests and the pharaoh took the small shrine with its statues inside the temple, where the pharaoh received divine blessings from the god Amen. Sometimes this entire journey and festival procession took place on boats that floated on the Nile between these two temples.

Farming Along the Nile

When the floodwaters receded from the lowlands, they replenished the farmland by leaving behind a rich coat of silt, or topsoil. This black soil was filled with nutrients such as nitrogen, which enriched the soil. The receding waters signaled the start of the annual season of rebirth and renewal. This was the time for farmers to go into their fields and plant their crops for the next year.

Planting conditions after the flood were perfect. The sun shone brightly, which was necessary for the growth of healthy, strong plants. Many inches of the soil, including the fertile top layer, were extremely muddy from the flood.

The mud made it easier for the farmers to plant their seeds. They didn't have to work a hoe through hard land or struggle to turn over their soil. They didn't have to water their fields once they planted their seeds. The flood did these chores for the farmers.

The farmers grew a wide variety of crops. They planted grains such as barley and wheat. They planted vegetables such as beans, chickpeas, cucumbers, lettuce, and onions. On higher land, the Egyptians created vineyards and orchards. The trees bore fruits such as pomegranates, figs, and dates. The farmers planted gardens of herbs and spices such as dill, thyme, sage, and cumin to flavor their food.

Many ancient Egyptians were farmers or herders.

Many animals were drawn to the Nile River, where they took refuge under the shade of palm trees and drank from the river. Ducks and geese waddled along the riverbanks or swam in the water. Fish, crocodiles, and hippopotamuses also made the river their home. All these creatures were hunted by the Egyptians.

Only the upper class and royalty could afford meals that included meat. The lower classes usually ate vegetarian meals, which they enjoyed with homemade bread. They spiced up their dishes with dill and cumin or sweetened them with honey. They also ate watermelon, grapes, figs, and dates.

The floodwaters also helped the Egyptians devise irrigation systems, which were important along the Nile River. The crops and orchards received plenty of sunlight, but they also needed a lot of water to produce an abundant harvest. The people needed water for drinking and bathing.

The Egyptians took advantage of natural **levees** created by rocks, dead trees, and debris from abandoned settlements. These objects were tossed into piles by the raging floodwaters. Once the water showed signs of receding, laborers ventured into the mud and propped up the piles to create sidewalls. They built the walls into networks of ditches and simple canals that trapped the water. Farmers used the trapped water to irrigate their crops. Other people used the water for their needs during the drier months.

The farmers also built their own canals to irrigate crops. These were especially important for their orchards and smaller gardens. As time went on, the irrigation systems became more complicated. The ancient Egyptians did their best to keep water flowing to their fields. Their hard work created large harvests that made Egypt a very rich kingdom.

These are the flowers of flax plants.

Many farmers and their families grew flax, which was used to produce linen. Linen was used to make clothing. This important plant was harvested while it was still blooming. Children piled the plants high on their heads. Adults with big bundles stacked in their arms carried the valuable plants from the fields to a flat area where the flax could dry out in the sun. Then women spun the fibers of the flax into thread that was woven into linen.

Ancient flax cord

Clothing was simple
and made of linen.

Egyptian Fashion

Clothing in ancient Egypt was relatively simple and
functional. Upper-class men usually wore short white skirts,
or kilts. Older men wore long comfortable robes that swept
down to their ankles.

Upper-class women dressed in close-fitting robes.
Sometimes they added a cape-style cloak over their
shoulders in the evenings, or if there was a rare cool breeze.
The women's hair, jewelry, and elaborate makeup, which
was especially dramatic around their eyes, held everyone's
attention, not their clothing.

Lower-class men and women wore kilts made of a
rougher linen. They were usually midcalf length. This
simple attire provided comfort and ease of movement when
they worked in the heat or in the fields. Children also wore
very simple kilts as they worked beside their parents.

Both sexes cared deeply about their appearance, especially members of the upper class. After they bathed, they dabbed on fragrant oils and creams to protect their skin from the dry heat.

Wealthy men and women spent a good deal of time grooming their hair. They rubbed it with wax from beehives, which held the style and made the hair shine. Many wealthy men and women, including the pharaohs, wore dark wigs designed in elaborate hairstyles.

The people of ancient Egypt loved jewelry. Men and women wore stone-studded metal collars and necklaces that draped down their necks. They wore wide cuffs of bronze, gold, and precious stones around their upper arms, wrists, and ankles. Their fingers sparkled with rings. So did their toes, which would peek out of their leather sandals.

For many centuries the Egyptians retained their customs, from their style of clothing to their religious beliefs. Their kingdom flourished along the Nile River. And for a long time, their civilization prospered.

Egyptians used combs and other objects to be fashionable.

Glossary

abundant *adj.* more than enough; very plentiful.

artifacts *n.* any items made by human skill or work, especially tools or weapons.

decrees *n.* decisions ordered by authority; laws.

eternity *n.* all time; an endless time period.

immortal *adj.* living forever, never dying, everlasting.

levees *n.* high banks built to keep a river from overflowing.

receded *v.* moved backward, withdrew.

reigned *v.* ruled over, as a monarch rules over a nation.